BERNARD LAZARE

THE MIRROR OF LEGENDS

TRANSLATED AND WITH AN INTRODUCTION BY
BRIAN STABLEFORD

THIS IS A SNUGGLY BOOK

ISBN: 978-1-943813-38-4

THE MIRROR OF LEGENDS

BERNARD LAZARE (1865–1903) was a French Jewish literary critic and journalist. Though mostly remembered today for his prominent role in the Dreyfus Affair and his book *Antisemitism: Its History and Causes*, he was also an important member of the Symbolist movement, and one of its purest and most extravagant exponents. He wrote drama and some poetry, but the core of his production consisted of an extensive sequence of short stories, or elaborated poems in prose, most of which he published in Symbolist periodicals between 1887 and 1893, and which he subsequently organized into three augmented collections. Although somewhat neglected today, for reasons that have nothing to do with their literary and philosophical merit, Lazare's short stories are key documents of the Symbolist movement, and a remarkable illustration of the methods and preoccupations of the writers whose activity constituted its heyday.

BRIAN STABLEFORD has been publishing fiction and non-fiction for fifty years. His fiction includes a series of "tales of the biotech revolution" and a series of metaphysical fantasies featuring Edgar Poe's Auguste Dupin. He is presently researching a history of French *roman scientifique* from 1700–1939 for Black Coat Press, translating much of the relevant material into English for the first time, and also translates material from the Decadent and Symbolist Movements. He has previously translated for Snuggly Books a number of titles, including *The Unknown Collaborator and Other Legendary Tales* by Victor Joly and *Bluebirds* by Catulle Mendès.

Contents

Introduction

L E MIROIR DES LÉGENDES by Bernard Lazare, here translated as *The Mirror of Legends*, was first published by Alphonse Lemerre in 1892. "Bernard Lazare" had been born Lazare Bernard on 14 June 1865 in Nîmes in the south of France, into a Jewish family long resident in the city. He had a secular education and was not much interested in the religious rituals of Judaism, cultivating an independence of thought that led him to look at his hereditary culture with a clinical and slightly jaundiced eye, but he was no positivist, always searching beyond dogmas for a more reliable and purified spirituality. Nor did his indifference to Jewish ritual prevent him from feeling the sting of anti-Semitism, to which he turned an equally clinical and similarly jaundiced eye, becoming sufficiently interested in it as a phenomenon to write an analytical history of it, *L'Antisémitisme, son histoire et ses causes* (1894; tr. as *Anti-Semitism, its History and its Causes*).

The objectivity of Lazare's approach inevitably attracted the hostility of the devout, which led to frequent accusations that he was anti-Semitic himself, in spite of the manifest absurdity of such a contention, given that the principal criticism he made of some of his fellow Jews was that of neglecting the spirituality of the faith in favor of an effective worship of "the beast" (the golden calf). Although he professed a great admiration for Christ and felt that the Jews were mistaken in rejecting him as the prophesied Messiah, he retained his allegiance to Judaism and Zionism. The mistaken charge did, however, hang over him to such an extent that all accounts of his life and work feel obliged to begin by confronting it; it dominates the early pages of Philippe Oriol's biography, *Bernard Lazare* (2003), along with the cause for which Lazare became famous as the pioneer and leading promoter: the Dreyfus Affair.

Lazare was one of the first and foremost champions of the unjustly-convicted Captain, and his journalistic activity was the poker that first invigorated its corrosive flames, following a savage article penned in 1896 that ended with a stark "J'accuse," a phrase subsequently appropriated by Émile Zola as the headline of his own assault. So important did the controversy over Dreyfus' fate become to the political conscience of France that it has come in retrospect to dominate Lazare's whole life, almost eclipsing everything else—except, of course, for the lingering suspicion of his alleged anti-Semitism, even though the root and branch of the Dreyfus Affair was a battle to expose and condemn the anti-Semitism that had initially condemned the Captain for an illusory crime and had then fought tooth and nail for years on end to defend that blatant injustice.

In fact, the Dreyfus Affair did largely take over Lazare's life while he was involved with it, and we do not know what he might have gone on to do once it was over, because by that time he was dying; his life came to a premature end on 1 September 1903, following an operation to remove a cancerous tumor from his bowel. Prior to his lighting the fuse of the Affair, however, Lazare had had a markedly different life and markedly different ambitions; he was a Symbolist, at the very heart of that literary movement, and one of its purest and most extravagant exponents. He wrote drama and some poetry, but the core of his production consisted of an extensive sequence of short stories, or elaborated poems in prose, most of which he published in Symbolist periodicals between 1887 and 1893, and which he subsequently organized into three augmented collections, *Le Miroir des légendes*, *Les Porteurs des torches* [*The Torch-Bearers*] (1897) and *Les Portes d'ivoire* [*The Ivory Gates*] (dated 1897, presumably having been assembled simultaneously with the previous item, but actually published in 1898).

Joris-Karl Huysmans once described the prose-poem as "the osmazome of literature," and although Symbolism was primarily a poetic movement, it is arguable that the poetry in prose the movement produced represents its truest essence. Almost all of the movement's leading practitioners, including Lazare's mentor Éphraïm Mikhaël (Éphraïm-Georges Michel), experimented with the form, but none did so quite as intensely and as determinedly as Lazare, and there is a sense in which his work in that vein does indeed contain and display the very essence of Symbolism, not merely in terms of its characteristic stylistic elaborations but also its rhetoric, its irony and its idealistic propaganda. *Le Miroir des légendes* is a perfect illustration of the latter, slightly hidden, agenda. In spite of the variety of its legendary sources, the collection as a whole has a remarkable rhetorical and thematic coherency, which goes far beyond the quasi-autobiographical frame provided by the first and last items, the remainder of the stories being carefully organized so as gradually to bring their constant preoccupations more evidently to the fore and into sharper focus.

Lazare was still living in the south of France in the mid-1880s when he began to correspond with Georges Michel, who was a year younger than him but was already beginning to publish his work in various periodicals under the adapted version of his name. Michel was a southerner like him, born into a Jewish family in Toulouse, but he went to Paris in 1883 to study at the Sorbonne, and settled there permanently, involving himself with a group of young poets, including Rodolphe Darzens, Pierre Quillard, "Saint-Pol-Roux" (Paul Pierre Roux) and René Ghil, and, most particularly, with his former English teacher Stéphane Mallarmé, whose *mardis* [Tuesday salons] were more reminiscent of a series of seminars in which the great man preached the Symbolist doctrine to his acolytes. Michel urged Lazare to come and join him, assuring him that it was absolutely necessary, if he wanted to be a poet, to be in Paris, and Lazare answered the call in October 1886, becoming his friend's right-hand man in the clique they formed, the "Moineaux francs" [house sparrows].

Unfortunately, the Moineaux francs did not last long, because its linchpin, Éphraïm Mikhaël, died of tuberculosis in May 1890, aged twenty-three, after a meteoric career during which he had published only three volumes, including a collaboration with Lazare, the drama *La Fiancée de Corinthe* [*The Bride of Corinth*] (1888), based on a legend recycled by Goethe. It was while he was in the clique as originally formed, however, that Lazare wrote almost all the stories collected in *Le Miroir des légendes*, and they are the product of that intellectual environment, hatched during Mallarmé's *mardis* under the aegis of that poet's esthetic theories, sometimes following exemplars established by other older writers appointed as heroes by the young Symbolists, especially Charles Leconte de Lisle, his fellow Parnassian, Léon Dierx and the legendary Comte de Villiers de l'Isle Adam.

The remainder of Mikhaël's band stayed in contact, although there was something of a split when some of them associated themselves with a new Symbolist periodical founded by Rémy de Gourmont and others the *Mercure de France*, while a minority, including Lazare, took the view that the niche market was already oversupplied and reserved their support for the existing periodicals, notably the *Revue bleue*, shunning the newcomer in a rather petty and self-defeating fashion.

In the meantime, however, Lazare had also become a regular attendee at other salons associated with the movement, most notably that hosted by José-Maria de Heredia, where the aged Leconte de Lisle still put in an occasional appearance. There he involved himself with another clique of young writers, whose central figures included Henri de Régnier—who was introduced to Heredia, his future father-in-law, by Mikhaël and Lazare—and Pierre Louÿs. He also met and befriended the woefully impoverished but still flamboyant Villiers de l'Isle Adam, not long before the latter's death. Like many of the members of the movement, but more fervently than most, Lazare also adopted the political philosophy of Anarchism in the 1890s—something else for which Oriol felt the need to mount an apologetic defense, although it would have been difficult to throw a stone into any fashionable *fin-de-siècle* Parisian literary salon without hitting a self-declared anarchist.

Lazare's family did not approve of his literary vocation, having planned a more orthodox career for him in the textile industry, in which his forefathers had long been active, and his relationship with them became somewhat strained after his relocation to Paris. That strain was further exaggerated because his family also disapproved strongly of his long-standing romantic liaison with Isabelle Grumbach, whom he had met in Nîmes when they were both teenagers, and which continued after he moved to Paris. Isabelle soon followed him there, enrolling at the Conservatoire and scraping together a meager living tinting photographs for Nadar's studio. Although their plans to marry were long frustrated by financial impracticality, they eventually managed to tie the knot in 1892; Lazare's family boycotted the wedding.

That relationship, too, forms part of the intellectual backcloth to the stories in *Le Miroir des légendes*, all of which were written while the marriage plans were in a state of reluctant suspension, and it is of some significance that Isabelle always was and remained until the end of his life Lazare's one and only love, whom he cherished very dearly. At least, he always said so, and continually proclaimed the fact in writing, although Oriol quotes a friend of the family who contended that he was never happy with her and that she neglected him shamefully while he was dying. That opinion might simply reflect the family's stubborn disapproval, but it is not inconceivable that Lazare was trying hard to convince himself of an ideal amour that reality could not sustain. To what extent some such psychology might be reflected in the stories is a matter for conjecture, but it is certainly the case that Lazare's work is distinct from that of most of the Symbolist writers in its attitude to amour, which is uncommonly straight-laced but also somewhat equivocal, and that odd combination—at its most graphically bizarre in "Les Fleurs" (tr. as "The Flowers")—adds a further dimension of fascination to them.

If the attitude to amour displayed by the stories in *Le Miroir des Légendes* is exceptional, so too, and even more so, is the attitude to death displayed therein. One of the most striking of the handful of stories based on Greek sources, "La Mort renoncée" (tr. as "Death Renounced"), is an elaboration of an allegation made by Cicero concerning the cynic philosopher Hegesias of Cyrene, which treats with unusual sympathy the probably false allegation that the philosopher in question preached the desirability of suicide so eloquently that he caused a virtual epidemic in Alexandria. A similar sentiment is echoed in more muted form in one or two other stories in the collection, but it is notable that almost all of them—ranging from the prehistoric fantasy "L'Offrande à la déesse" (tr. as "The Offering to the Goddess") to the exceedingly peculiar futuristic fantasies "Les Incarnations" (tr. as "The Incarnations") and "In Excelsis," via the tales based in scriptural and Greek legend—feature heroic, tragic and ironic deaths, and a preoccupation with sacrifice and martyrdom bordering on obsession.

It is perhaps not surprising that Lazare's Symbolist work should manifest a certain preoccupation with death, given that the example of Villiers de l'Isle Adam's miserable demise in 1889 was followed within a year by Mikhaël's tragic end, which must have been obviously impending in the interim. If the stories are a partial reflection of his manner of dealing with those losses psychologically, however—

and, indeed, part and parcel of that mental contention—
they are certainly idiosyncratic, evidently fused in some
instances with his parallel contention with Judaism and his
own quest for a special spirituality, which becomes strik-
ingly innovative in the far-reaching "L'Agonie des esprits
(tr. as "The Agony of the Spirits").

Although somewhat neglected today, for reasons that
have nothing to do with their literary and philosophical
merit, Lazare's three collections of short stories are key
documents of the Symbolist movement, and a remarkable
illustration of the methods and preoccupations of the
writers whose activity constituted its heyday. Hopefully, it
will be possible for the present volume to be followed up
by translations of *Les Porteurs de torches* and *Les Portes d'ivoire*,
provided that I and the publisher live long enough.

This translation was made from the copy of the Lemerre
edition reproduced on the Bibliothèque Nationale's *gallica*
website.

Brian Stableford

THE MIRROR OF LEGENDS

The Garden

But my desire always goes toward the mystery,
Of marvelous lands where I have never set foot.

Éphraïm Mikhaël.

THE garden has not sealed mysterious Avalons and white Thules forever; the doors are not irredeemably closed.

You who, in the troubling pleasures of pale visions, flee the cities where you dragged your heart, your poor darkened heart; you who are weary of banal voices, quit the noisy crowds and sonorous voids and travel on roads detestable to you; you will find the garden of mysterious Avalons and white Thules.

If you are fond of abolished glories, if you have spat on the festivals in which, drunk on malign liquors, your brothers are feasting; if your dream is distant; if your desires are noble; extend your feeble hands even so; be fearless, and the magical beasts that guard the thresholds of fortunate countries will lick your feet and open the way for you to Thules and Avalons.

If your soul is pure, its own light will guide you, far from the borders that pollute the false pilgrims, through the bushes where large venomous flowers bloom for the impious, toward the bolted doors guarded by dragons, chimeras and wyverns, toward the doors of Avalons and Thules.

Then, behind rugged walls bristling with spikes, you will perceive the quivering crowns of friendly trees. The leaves of their branches sparkle, like candid enamels, and their gleam will be soft. The indulgent foliage will spread its subtle aromas over you; the scattered benevolent odors will lull all your senses, and the clement murmur of the soon-conquered forest will salute the new lover of Avalons and Thules.

And you will hear the song of virgins who walk in the shade of hasty rose-bushes, while invisible birds celebrate infallible joys in puerile cantilenas. Listen to the virgins who walk in the shade of hasty rose-bushes, the virgins of Thules and Avalons.

"Welcome, voyager, undervalued voyager! For you our fraternal voices have resonated, you have replied to our evocative appeal. You have groaned along evil paths; captive on the banks of enemy rivers, you have suffered. Our frail fingers have brushed your forehead with bright corollas, and those exiles have announced fabulous dreamlands to you. You are worn out, like a fawn tracked by hunters, and we read the customary apprehensions and fears in your still-obscure soul.

"Have no fear; you have already crossed the invisible porticos that the profane will never reach.

"Come to us, the revealers. You have left the impure gold, the sordid mire; henceforth you shall have unexperienced delights. You have disdained abject acclamations, and have rejected the buccinas of base triumphs; you have renounced the consecratory pedestals of unhealthy renown: you will contemplate your eternal and true image in the mirror of pure lakes.

"Come! Here the softness of lawns is starred with strange calices, the branches of orchards are hung with glistening fruits, melodious perfumes take flight, and rippling streams proffer unheard words.

"Come! An undulating and peaceful light will caress your eyes; look: it has the infantile candor of auroras, the attractive melancholy of dusks, the infinite gentleness of blue twilights.

"Come! You will know the eternity of the Word. The golden sistra are ready, the strings vibrate beneath the plectra, the air quivers with latent speech, rhythms are dormant in the wind, thoughts are huddled in the depths of grottoes.

"Enter, you will awaken the world that is waiting for you."

Thus you will hear the virginal spinners who tread the scattered moss beneath the blooming roses: the spinners of Avalons and Thules.

Touch, with your intrepid finger, the emerald that seals the heavy battens, and the battens will open. See, it is palpitating, the unpolluted gem; it is calling to you: "You whose soul is pure, aching heart, hear me! Hear me, new lover fond of abolished glories! The doors are not irredeemably closed; it is never closed, the garden of mysterious Avalons and white Thules."

The Offering to the Goddess

To Camille Bloch.[1]

Echo of great primitive evenings.
J. Laforgue.[2]

TWICE already, covered by its thick shroud of ice, the young globe had gone to sleep; twice it had wandered through space, cold and wan. One day, centuries ago, it had shaken its white cope, and now, crowned with forest tresses, the earth smiled again in the dawns, and quivered mysteriously in the dusks. But beneath the woods of beeches and oaks, the grave tread of the mammoth with the silky fleece was no longer heard; the ancient colossi were all dead; dead the heavy mastodons and the gigantic rhinoceroses; dead the enormous tigers and the prodigious bears. Slowly, the wapiti and the reindeer retreated toward the poles; the lions and the leopards went in search

---

1 Camille Bloch (1865–1949), a historian, was the archivist of the Aude when the present collection was published.

2 Jules Laforgue (1860–1887) was a Symbolist poet and an important precursor of Surrealism, whose premature death robbed the Chat Noir generation of one of its brightest stars. His *Moralités légendaires* (1887) includes some stories of a similar genre to those in *Le Miroir des légendes*, but more elaborate and extravagant.

of warmer climes. Only the aurochs with thick horns remained in these valleys, with the elk and the red deer.

Humans from the East had subjugated the old races. Tall blond people with long heads, broad foreheads and bright eyes ruled Europe; they lived in profound caves and sometimes built towns on the waters of blue lakes.

It was evening.

The sun was descending toward the horizon, brushing the skies with its bloody flowers, and its declining rays deposited sparkling bands of gold, rutilant with cinnabar, on the hills; in the east, white clouds spread out their carpet; here and there, light snowflakes floated as if in a lake. The blue of the firmament, ardent near the luminous nucleus, passed from deep lapis lazuli to pale sapphire and extinct gray, dotted with red and yellow clouds, sometimes giving birth to monstrous islands the color of bright rust, which darkened, elongated and changed shape, reminiscent of long serpents covered in brown scales.

Meanwhile, the star sank on to a bed of violet mist, and in the distance, the darkness was already displaying its black veil. Tenuous vapors, which sublimated as they reached the heights, rose from the meadows. Beneath the foliage of obscure forests, vague noises shivered; first there was birdsong, timid notes, sketched trills, frail piping and interrupted clucking; then stags belled, the lowing of oxen and the whinnying of horses was heard, and above those voices resounded the laughter of hyenas and the yapping of jackals.

The people of the tribe had quit their rocky shelters; they were squatting on the ground and, with their elbows on their knees, supporting their heads in their hands, their eyes fixed and haggard, they watched the dazzling orb disappear. As if devoured by an invisible monster, the disk was rapidly eaten away; then it threw off brilliant rockets, agonizing in an ocean of blood. The terrified women cried out, extending their arms toward the flamboyant cavalier, to appeal to him and hold him back—but the king was vanquished; one last time he launched a sigh of flame, and then he disappeared, while the pink gleams flew into the empyrean. The old men uttered a plaintive groan, and for a long time the entire horde, prostrate, wept for the dead sun.

Now night enveloped the forests; its black waves had submerged the floating clarities, and even the luminous down gilding the mountain peaks had vanished; no spark palpitated over the somber verdure of the pines scaling the slopes. The birdsong had ceased, the horses and the familiar oxen had lain down in the grass, and the stags were no longer belling in the clearings; only the plaints of the hyenas burst forth, and suddenly the dogs, guardians of the herds, began to howl. Arranged in a circle, spines arched, legs agitated by tremors, necks extended, mouths drooling, they ululated lugubriously, their sobs casting gloom over the heights and the plains, the meadows and the woods.

Like an agonized appeal, the lamentable cries sounded, spreading terror; and yet, the pale and trembling beings cowering on the ground stood up with a clamor of joy. On the horizon, the moon had just appeared, opening her red eye. Clarity was reborn.

Then, two young men having given the signal by crashing round stones together, the tribe marched away. First came the chiefs, clad in fabrics made from linen bark; they had staffs of reindeer horn pierced with holes, the insignia of their dignity; on their heads glittered nets covered with nacreous shells; their breasts were ornamented with ivory plaques, and over their bellies hung symbolic triangles made of red porphyry or green jade. Next came the warriors, covered by the skins of wild beasts. They were armed with javelins tipped with sharpened flint, daggers with flat and diamond-shaped hilts, and arrows whose polished stone heads were encased in deer-antlers. Some were brandishing smooth barbed lances; others preferred serpentine, jasper or simple quartz axes; a few could even be seen who carried clubs in the shape of cockleshells, carved in white granite speckled with black mica. All of them were protected by precious amulets; there were pierced teeth, crescents raising their obsidian horns, bizarrely engraved strips of schist, and most of all, roundels cut out of human skulls.

In the rearguard, the women had been placed. They were clad in short garments of linen, with fringes, and adorned with numerous items of jewelry. The majority wore ornaments composed of gray and light-brown shells, two pairs falling in the middle of the forehead, two surrounding each arm, four circling the knees and two displayed on the feet. The richest wore rings, pendants and bracelets for which alabaster, callais[1] and yellow amber had been worked, necklaces in jet or violet fluorine, the pearls of which were round or cylindrical, elongated like spindles or sculpted into double cones. The old men and children remained under the guard of the most valiant men.

They went northwards. Rapidly, they traversed the meadows bathed with the bleached light of the moon, and, when they had been marching for an hour, they

---

1 Callais is a green stone found in Neolithic beads and ornaments.

stopped in a circular valley surrounded by bald hills. In the middle of the circle was the entrance to a cave; to the right and left of the opening, two menhirs raised up their rigid masses, meaning the heavens. Already-numerous groups were squatting around it. Gradually, the valley filled up. Confused rumors rose up from the crowd; all eyes turned toward the stone colossi. Suddenly, a muffled noise resounded in the grotto; a mysterious terror passed over the valley; heads bowed; the crypt was illuminated; an old man appeared on the threshold. He made a sign, and, slowly and silently, the people went in.

They went through a vestibule devoid of ornaments and entered a vast chamber. The walls, carefully polished, were decorated with designs: bizarrely tangled arabesques, parallel lines and others that were divergent met one another and intersected one another, and the symbolic triangle appeared everywhere. Lamps hung from the vault, made of earthenware, and cups rounded like eggs or skulls; in the middle, a schist crescent was suspended.

At the back of the lair stood the goddess. She was sculpted in a block of white granite; her eyes were made with two black pearls; she had a bird's beak and pointed breasts. Her bosom was ornamented with a large necklace carved in the block, with an encased amber cylinder at its center. To the right and left of the divinity were two enormous axes; above, in the rock, in elevated relief, an ill-formed statue of a woman was visible, her legs immodestly open; below, a long stone lay, narrow and rectangular, pitted with cupules representing vaginas, connected by a furrow. Further down, a porphyry table had been set.

One by one, in order of preeminence, the men sat down on the ground: the chiefs in the first row, then the warriors; the women were crowded under the portico. The old man who had led them stood in front of them; he took hold of a vase; he drank slowly, and the myrtle wine was passed around. Then the first, the eldest, turned to the sacred bird and uttered a bizarre clamor. Strange moans emerged from the crowd; in a mysterious language, everyone chanted hymns, measuring the words rhythmically, unfurling litanies.

Gradually, they became agitated, their cries became shriller, more violent; convulsions shook their limbs; their faces were disfigured by ecstatic grimaces; and abruptly, a young man launched himself forward. He lay face down before the goddess, remained immobile momentarily, then got up and went to lie on the porphyry table. The old man approached him; with his right hand he took a long flint knife, with his left he seized the hair of the voluntary victim; the weapon glinted, the man stood up, circled by a bloody tonsure, and the sacrificer brandished the red roundel.

The howls of the faithful redoubled; a warrior presented himself. Already, when younger, he had offered himself, and the yawning gap in his skull attested his faith; he prostrated himself at the feet of the idol, surrendered himself to the old man and got up again crowned with a red diadem, while the crowd cheered. Then there was madness. They precipitated themselves forward in dense columns, and the first alone adored the image, the others being in haste to have the rutilant blade plunge into their brains.

The strong brutally made room, the weak could not reach the altar and lamented plaintively or rolled on the ground, foaming at the mouth and writhing; some even smashed their skulls against the walls. The ancestor's arm fell and rose, stained red; an insipidly acrid odor filled the chamber; fuming blood spread out in a black sheet over the ground; the devotees with soiled hair bent lower down. And that lasted for a long time; for hours the holocausts presented themselves freely; the immolator felt weary.

But the lamps sputtered, a pale ray of light slid into the cavern, the initial sound burst forth again; the sacrifice ceased, the vociferations of the women announced the renascent star, and they all went out to greet the day.

They extended their arms toward the east; in a prodigious enthusiasm they danced, glad to see the god they had thought dead live again. Their clamors of joy resounded in the valley. They forgot the bleak moon and the evil divinity, avid for palpitating flesh; even those whose wounds were dolorous were trembling, singing with ardor, and no longer felt their wounds, for the new light had abolished their suffering. In the same order in which they had come, they left the valley.

Shivering with an immense delight, they went through the meadows embalmed with balsamic effluvia, though the forests where awakening creatures were murmuring, and, without dread, they marched beneath the rising sun.

The Eternal Fugitive

To Émile Vermeil.[1]

Nunc igitur maledictus eris super terram
                                        Genesis.[2]

I

THEY had moaned in servitude, they had built pyramids and cities, during the years they had bent their backs under the whip of the Egyptians. Then, Yahveh having awakened, they had girded their loins for the journey and, the lamb having been sacrificed, they had fled, in the midst of miracles, amid rains of blood and filthy animals. At the voice of their guide, horses and riders were engulfed in the red flood and, for the three months that they wandered in the desert, their murmurs rose up, for they were a stiff-necked people; but they were about to encounter God.

---

1 Émile Vermeil published a short monologue called "Pauvre Pierrot" in the Symbolist periodical *L'Ermitage* in 1890, following a stage reading, but history seems to have lost sight of him otherwise.
2 From the Lord's injunction to Cain in the Vulgate version of *Genesis* 4:11; the A.V. renders it as "And now art thou cursed from the earth."

At the foot of Sinai they now set up their tents, mute in the anguish of theophanies, and terror made their hair bristle. Uncrossable limits had been set for them; no one was to touch the borders of the holy mountain, and the cadavers of violators already strewed the ravines, men and dogs struck by arrows or stones.

To the sound of trumpets, in the midst of smoke and flames, Yahveh had descended to the summit of the mountain; he had summoned Moses, and Moses had gone to him. On the arid slopes of Sinai, Aaron, Nabab and Abihou, with seventy elders, awaited the prophet, and the people languished, lamenting.

The Hebrews forgot the services rendered, the scourges sent and their deliverance; terrified by the sound of thunder and the clamor of clarions, they felt alone, abandoned by their leaders, deprived by God; and the days passed, the nights dragged by slowly, and forty went by thus.

Rumors ran through the crowd. Men attached in spite of everything to the gods of Mizraim, accused Sabaoth of having deceived them. They went into the camp, and went into the tents; they murmured in the ears of women that if they were obstinate in waiting for the son of Jochebed they would perish in the waterless sands. They mingled with the consternated groups and proclaimed the death of Moses.

"The one," they said, "who has already drawn into an ambush the spouse of blood, has struck him irrevocably this time, and he will never reappear in the midst of his people."

Some, elders instructed by innumerable days of servitude, resisted the evil insinuations. They insulted the traitors, threatened them with the divine wrath ready to afflict them with hideous ulcers and frightful leprosies. The rebels scoffed at them, and the people, not seeing the promised punishments come, turned against the old men. They were jeered when they wanted to speak, they were covered with coarse mockery and their beards were tugged ironically. They did not shut up, however, and their execrations resounded incessantly in hoarse voices. Then people spat in their faces, beat them with rods, and one of them even died from the blows—and no punishing thunderbolt emerged from the mountain crowned with flames.

"Yahveh!" cried the women. "Knavish God, you have abandoned us. You said to us: 'You are my children, I will guide you to friendly lands, I will heap you with goods there.' Is this the prosperity that you promised the patriarchs? Why do you render our wombs fecund if it be only to dry up our breasts? Could you not have left us on the banks of the river, in the land of sycamores, instead of leading us here, into these morose deserts, where we shall die of hunger and thirst?"

And the men, troubled by these lamentations, wept. They regretted Mizraim, the vines buckling under the weight of grapes, and the muddy plains covered in crops; they forgot the days of rude labor, only remembering the luminous nights when, under the swaying leaves of palm trees, they rested next to wives with tempting loins; then their amorous sighs mingled with the winds that brought the date-palms the male seeds, and they engendered, lulled by the cadence of blue waves perfumed by lotus blossom.

When their despair had abated, when they had understood the inanity of their regrets, they blasphemed the deceiver Adonai. They showed their fists to the tempestuous mountain where trumpets resounded, they threw stones at it, they heaped their Lord with reproaches, and, as they could not remain alone, they demanded another Elohim with loud cries. They would have adopted those of their former masters, but they did not know whether Ptah or Osiris would come to them, frankly, and they scorned the goddesses: maternal Isis, Neith and Sekhmet with the head of a lioness. Their fury at being abandoned by Yahveh was augmented by the fear of not finding a god who wanted to receive them.

Then, from among Israel, a man stood up, whose name was Samiri.[1] Few knew him, for he lived in solitude; there were some who had never seen him, and some who even said that he was not of the race of Abraham. He advanced toward the anxious multitude, and everyone fell silent in order to listen to him.

"You want a god," he said, "and like you, I want one, since ours, belying his promises, has fled from us. But we need a lord faithful to his people, not a tyrant who unleashes his anger, like a dromedary among the furrows. Have you not bowed down under the rod of Yahveh?"

At that name, furious cries and blasphemies emerged from the crowd, and when they fell silent, Samiri continued:

"Let us make a god in accordance with our desires, whom we will break if he does not obey our prayers; a god whom we can carry; a god who is a prisoner of his servants; a god who will tremble before the threats of the Levites and the maledictions of his people; a god viler

---

1 Samiri is the name given in the Quran to the creator of the golden calf; in *Exodus* 32 it is made by Aaron.

than us, impotent to vanquish us or to humiliate us with his grandeur."

The joyful Hebrews acclaimed the man; they held out their hands to him and they all prayed:

"Samiri, make us a god!"

II

At the foot of the mountain, on a high-set altar palpitating with holocausts, the golden calf was erected, sparkling, bathed with aromatics, haloed with sacred perfumes. To cast it, the warriors had given Samiri their earrings, the maidens and the wives had let the jewelry fall from their hair and arms. When the Beast had emerged from the mold, everyone had thrown themselves face down before it, to worship their impure work, and now, slumped around the tables, they were eating, drinking and amusing themselves, while, their hair dirty and their clothing torn, the Levites were weeping silently, their faces covered.

A special delight penetrated the people; they felt liberated from respect. Far away, very far away, was the fear of the divine that incites meditations; the fear that provokes prayers had disappeared; souls, freed from specious doubts, understanding their god, no longer needed to think; bodies, liberated from customary and henceforth fallacious dreads, were able to enjoy. Thus, at table in the camp, filthy words and obscene songs were heard resounding.

Gorged with nourishment, drunk on wine, the men were relieving themselves noisily, and rolling in their vomit without shame. Before the exalted brute, they interlaced, immodestly, complicating the soiling, mingling Gomorrah, Sodom and the sins of other cities. Those who had remained seated at the feast threw pieces of meat at the idol, and they all shuddered with an unprecedented and prodigious joy, for they could insult a god, freely.

<h1 style="text-align:center">III</h1>

However, the days having gone by, the man who had seen the Eternal face to face came down the mountain, holding the tablets on which the law was inscribed. In the distance, he heard the cries, and he made haste, believing that the Hebrews were calling to him. Suddenly he stopped, standing on a rock that overhung the desert; his eyes, which the glory of Yahveh had been unable to dazzle, closed; he had seen the golden calf, and a heavy silence fell upon the plain; the crowd had seen the prophet. The Levites who were lamenting stood up and came toward Moses, but Moses, with a great gesture of execration, broke the tablets; he raised his arm toward the Beast, and the Beast collapsed, in a proud flamboyance.

Until nightfall, in the tents, those who had remained faithful to Yahveh killed, and they did not spare their sons, nor their wives, nor any of those who were traitors to the liberator god. When the sun had closed its indifferent eye behind the red waves of sand, Moses made the survivors drink bitter waters that contained the dust of the idol; he had Samiri brought before him, and, the Lord illuminating him with his wisdom, he spoke:

"It is you again," he said, "and since the fault, the first after the primordial, since the chastisement, you have not been pardoned by Elohim."

"No," replied Samiri. "I am like him; I remember offences, and it is not yet your foot that will crush me, son of Jochebed; your stammering does not frighten me."

"I have recognized you," continued the Inspired, "you who have wandered since the day when, on the fuming altar, you felled Abel. Why have you come back to these people, you who were expelled by them?"

"What does it matter?" said the man. "Why are you interrogating me? We are not of the same race and your laudatory speech would go poorly with my voice. Slave, conductor of slaves, continue your route; for myself, I shall follow mine, and the malediction of which your mouth is full will not aggravate my destiny. For a moment I wanted to sympathize with the woes of Israel, and I gave the children of your master the only god that suits them. Henceforth, you will instruct them vainly, and if terror makes them bow their heads before Yahveh, they will retain in their soul the image that my fingers kneaded. Now, speak, my lips will not open again to respond. I am waiting."

"Go," cried Moses. "Go far away from the designated tribes. Flee, forever a vagabond, as the Eternal has willed, and let your new blasphemy increase the horror around you. Go away! If some, ignorant of your sins, want to welcome you, tell them, instrument of your own justice, not to approach you, and that no one, sympathetic or savage, should touch your abject flesh with a caress, or even a blow.

"And you, Hebrews, listen to me. You have come toward the one whom the Cherubim once punished, you have listened to his advice, and yet, the benevolent Lord has chastised you and not annihilated you. But woe betide you if you renew the fault—and you will, alas, renew it! A time will come when the criminal will choose a domicile beside your dwellings again, and no Levite, then, will stand up to repel him. One somber morning, out there in the promised Canaan, the accursed one who still mocks his master will strike the one who, bearing the cross, will climb the hill; then your laughter will salute his last mockery, and in your hearts, you will think as he does. On that day, you will be abandoned by your father; he will winnow you in the wind of his fury; he will disperse you over the earth, like grains of wheat impotent to take root; the veil will be torn from your sanctuaries; you will be a dead nation, and the world will be lost to you forever."

Having spoken those words, the Seer wept for a long time for his people, and then he climbed the mountain where the angry Yahveh was waiting for him. In the camp, the men groaned like fawns who fear the inevitable hunter; their unquiet eyes followed Moses, surrounded by flames, but sometimes, furtively, they turned their heads, and with regretful sighs, they watched the solitary Samiri, who was drawing away into the desert.

The Key to the Enigma

To Pierre Quillard.[1]

What does it matter to you?
I know the word, the charm, the sign.
Henri de Régnier.[2]

NOW, in order to escape the oracle, Oedipus was exiled from Corinth, abandoning the palace saddened by his sin, along with the old man Polybus and Queen Merope. His eyes filled with horror, shivering at the thought of the crime ineluctably predicted by the God, he had wandered the roads, haggard. One morning, at the hour when dawn illuminates the hillsides, in the shadowed valley where three roads met, he had chastised the insolent ancestor who had insulted him, and then, his eyes still fixed on the stars, he had continued his vagabond course, going toward the lands where he could laugh at destiny.

However, the soul of the divine ancestors lived in his

---

1 Pierre Quillard (1864–1912) was a core member of the clique formed around Éphraïm Mikhaël (a former classmate of his) and Lazare; like the latter he became an ardent Dreyfusard and fervent anarchist.
2 Henri de Régnier (1864–1936) was one of the leading Symbolist poets and prose writers of the *fin-de-siècle*, who enjoyed a long and successful career thereafter.

soul; the son of a king, he dreamed of a glorious future; he thought that a throne was due to him, and those heroic dreams made him forget for a moment the words heard before the fatal tripod.

When he learned about the misfortunes of Thebes; when, near a spring, a shepherd told him about the murder of Laius, the vengeances of the sphinx that ate human flesh, and the promises of Jocasta, he thought that he ought to deliver the city of the seven gates, in order to become the spouse of a sovereign and the master of the ancient Kadmeions.

He retired to the depths of the forest, and for days and nights, sleeping on dry leaves, taking no nourishment, only drinking a few mouthfuls of water, he reflected on the Enigma and the key that would vanquish the winged Virgin.

The aegipans and the hamadryads, hidden behind the oaks, spied on the somber dreamer with a vague fear. In the woods, solemnized by that thought, trying to get a grip on themselves, the goat-foots dared not pursue the nymphs; everything fell silent around the man, for the invisible gods were gradually illuminating his mind, destined by inviolable laws to penetrate the mystery.

One evening, a satyr saw Oedipus' eyes suddenly shine, and glimpsed a smile on his lips, and when the sun rose, the seeker quit his retreat and headed for Thebes.

Indifferently, he neglected Megara, he crossed the Kithairon dear to Dionysus, he drank the water of the Asopos, and after having traversed the Beotian plains, he saw the Kadmeia rising up in the auroral mists, the old citadel that had once contemplated the Heliconides singing the marriage of Harmonia and Kadmos. Mount

Sphyngios, the guardian of the Ogygian city, appeared to him, at the summit of which crouched the enchantress with the body of a beast. Oedipus scaled the height.

When he had reached the summit, the Sphinx loomed up before him, but the inflexible eyelids of the hero did not droop. He sustained without trembling the shock of the redoubtable pupils, so he did not perceive, on the ground, the bones of those who had perished at the monster's feet in the audacious effort of the climb: some of them fallen while trying to kiss the lips of the charmer; others torn apart while embracing her pointed breasts; these crushed when they leapt on to her back; and those struck dead at the supreme moment when their fingers brushed her hair.

Upright, the son of kings was still waiting, and the Virgin spoke, in a pale voice devoid of timbre or authority:

"There is still time for you, Unknown. If, more heroic than ordinary mortals, you have been able to sustain my gaze without being frightened, you will not resist the horror of the question posed, and like those who have preceded you, you will perish. Go away! For you, perhaps, splendid dawns might shine and consoling dusks fade away; flee over the fields without turning your head; do not tempt me."

Intrepidly, the seeker replied: "I await your demand, O Virgin; I have thought for a long time, and I am no longer afraid."

"You have wanted it, Stranger." The heavy syllables fell through the air; they appeared to descend from unknown spheres and not the Being, whose mouth was agitated nevertheless.

"Who am I?" the Sphinx interrogated "Exceedingly subtle diviner, penetrate my essence. Pronounce the word that will make me tell you the final secret."

Oedipus looked at the city that was awakening in the distance, the towers displayed there, rutilant in the sunlight, the white frontons of the temples and the tombs of illustrious warriors. Then, very calmly, he said:

"Evil immolatrice, you are no one, and no mystery has been confided to you. One day, you spoke, affirming that you were the depository of the ineffable Enigma, and candid humans believed you, for it was pleasant to hear the existence proclaimed of their perpetual ideal. Wearied by their vain research, they came to you with anxious souls, and their brothers were not astonished not to see the bold voyagers again. Now you have made enough victims; it is time to talk. It is necessary that credulous mortals recognize the inanity of their belief. They ought to know that their blind faith alone created your power. And henceforth, liberated from the deceptive hope of victory, they will march resignedly toward the goal that they glorify perpetually; for, fallacious instigator, I, the elect of mortals, have come to tell you that your deified, worshipped lie is your only strength; your secret is that you have no secret."

The words of the man resonated like a trumpet call; they resounded in the plain, and the inhabitants of the city heard them. They came out in a crowd, filling the squares. With a joyful fear they saw the killer, whom they had believed to be immortal, disappear like an illusory appearance, vanishing without leaving a misty trace, and they acclaimed the hero who remained alone on Mount Sphyngios.

When the tamer of the prophetess came down from the mountain, the maidens came to meet him, bearing palms and flowers. They held out their grateful hands toward him, and, after having saluted the King, they led him no Thebes.

Thus fell the Sphinx, and it was inevitable, for, by virtue of an eternal will, it was necessary that the fatal Labdakide[1] know his mother's bed and engender fraternal sons.

1 Labdakide, a collective term for the second royal dynasty of Thebes, is more familiar in German sources than French, but it is used in Leconte de Lisle's translation of *Oedipus Rex*, from which Lazare presumably took it.

The Sacrifice

To F. Herold.[1]

Myself, I curse that dolorous moment
That gave me life in order to be unhappy.
André Chenier.[2]

I

IT was near the city, Calydon the marine, in a silent wood, the last trees of which expired on the strand where the waves came to die, that Coresos had encountered Callirhoe for the first time.[3] And in him, the memory had remained unabolished of that calm evening where the gold of ripe oranges bathed in the powder of a gold more intense: the marvelous and essential gold of the sun, caressing with a last intoxication of radiance the bloody summits of waves and branches, which sank down weeping in the ancient

1 André-Ferdinand Herold (1865–1940) was the grandson of the composer Ferdinand Herold (1791–1833). He attended Mallarmé's *mardis* and Heredia's salon, where Lazare probably met him.
2 The poet André Chenier (1762–1794) was an important precursor of the Romantic Movement, reckoned as one of French literature's greatest losses to the Revolutionary guillotine.
3 The story of Coresos and Callirhoe can be found in Pausanias' *Description of Greece*; Lazare's version is a straightforward expansion.

and yet renascent dolor of the death of light.

From that day on, Coresos had forgotten the temple and the god of whom he was the priest, and had he not had the habit, still cherished, that had bowed him down since childhood at the feet of the customary altars, he would have neglected King Bacchus for the Anadyomene on whom, whether or not she wanted to be the auxiliary of his growing amour, his life depended henceforth.

He had followed the young woman everywhere. In the middle of processions of maidens going to springs, he had admired her svelte attitude, he had coveted the marmoreal softness of her body, as it inclined toward the undulating mirror, and of her arms, whose indecisive gestures sustained flowers. Then, one evening, having joined her near the sea, he had told her that he loved her. She had laughed, the ironic laugh of a beautiful child, while her foot pushed pebbles in the sand like silver coins by virtue of their pallor; and yet, weary rather than tender, she had allowed him to take from her girdle a rose whose whiteness was softened around a core enlivened by bright yellow.

Like all lovers, Coresos had desiccated the rose beneath incessant kisses, and then, when the last petal, in dying, had lost the perfume that seemed to him to come from his beloved, he wanted to see Callirhoe again. On a similar evening, before the same foaming waves, he told her again that he adored her and that death would be sweeter to him than life without her. This time, Callirhoe did not reply. She bent down, picked up with her slow fingertips the quivering feather of a pigeon that was skimming the scattered shells of whelks, and, with a breath, sent it flying over the sea. Coresos seized the feather, already wet, and fled, weeping, turning his head toward the woman who was no longer gazing at him.

Soon, his passion, irritated by disdain and magnified by indifference, dominated his mind, which rendered one single and invasive thought demented. As he had always been chaste, lustful images haunted his life, and with obscene processions, once purely followed, he mingled the precise vision of Callirhoe. He dared not approach the young woman again, the memory of the unfortunate encounter being too painful, but he loved to walk, far behind her, along the familiar pathways of his dreams, as far as the edge of the wood.

In her wake, he penetrated beneath the foliage yellowed by light; benevolently, the complicit shade of pomegranates and tall laurier-roses hid him from gazes; the ground, which the amorous humidity of the trees softened, muffled his footfalls, and he was able to contemplate Callirhoe, who went on pensively, sometimes leaning toward the suspended clusters of privet, or reaching up, her hand extended avidly, for a fruit lacerated with crimson.

Often, she paused. The seductive shadow of a bushier arbor, the incitation of thicker grass, and perhaps also the lassitude of the silence, the enveloping languor that the forest allows to fall over its limbs, made her collapse in a nonchalant pose soon immobilized by slumber. Then Coresos drew closer, and he watched her sleep, fearful of a licentious aegipan, whose back he thought he glimpsed in the mossy roughness of an oak, even fearing a malicious hamadryad, who presence he suspected every time that the aromatic scent of the foliage spread out more strongly. When a quiver, revelatory of an imminent awakening, agitated the sleeper, he hid again under the cover of a thicket, and as in coming, he followed Callirhoe on her return, with the same joy that a single regret, perpetually the same, rendered bitter afterwards.

One morning, however, the young woman encountered him near a temple and as he stood before her very humbly, without being able to find, in order to say it to her, the word that he repeated constantly, she spoke to him. In brief sentences slightly ironic with regard to the timid infatuation that he had, she revealed to him the vanity of his pursuits, his everyday pilgrimages, supported every day, which she now found tedious, as tedious as his affection. She declared to him that she would never have any love for him. Even tolerance of the languorous confessions and distant homages thus far manifest, tacit acclamations of her beauty, not excessive but agreeable, she no longer wanted to support. It displeased her to see exaggerated a passion of which she was the non-participant object, and cruel words followed, driving to despair the miserable lover whom she quit, haughtily insensible, without the alms of a gesture, or even a gaze.

After that conversation, Coresos remained mournful and sad for several weeks, distraught with the alarm of the dreams tragically renounced; then, his chagrin, which time delivered from the fatal excess of the first hours, began to reason. He was penetrated by the incomprehensible injustice of his fate, and, if he had initially excused Callirhoe by detailing, in an overly scrupulous fashion, the ugliness and the vices that he thought he had discovered in himself momentarily, he came, gradually, to think that only the virginal cruelty of the chosen one was culpable. Desires for vengeance soon obsessed him, and he remembered that he was a priest of a powerful God, who never failed his own.

He found subtle prayers to implore Bacchus, in which repentance for the recent abandonment was mingled with the desire to see realized the wish that had brought him back to the neglected cult. Propitiatory sacrifices appeased his remorse and rendered more accessible the triumphant king whose help he expected; so Coresos redoubled his invocations and the ejaculatory requests, which he finally saw granted. The one who dominated intoxications, the ordinator of symbolic phalalogies,[1] the master of the agitated bacchantes, showed himself to be angered by the insult made to the worshiper whose penitence touched him, and he, who had by his sovereign will driven insane a king once outrageously proud, struck the city with dementia.

II

There was, among the rare Calydonians who were spared, a profound desolation at the unexpected arrival of the scourge. The abnormal conduct of the wisest in the city, who were preferentially seized, caused a terror that complicated the invincible laughter provoked by the strange attitudes and extravagant words of the delirious. The irreverent actions of young men and the illicit conduct of maidens, which attracted the realizations of obscene dreams scarcely suspected by decrepit old men, were frightening by virtue of their inclusive and comprehensive necessity. The will, albeit a trifle facetious, of a redoubtable Olympian, seemed palpably inevitable, and the ritual

---

1 I have transcribed this term as it appears in the original, although it might well be a misprint for phallogies, which would presumably refer to phallic symbols.

supplications, like the customary holocausts of benevolent receptions, proved inefficacious.

Thus was imposed the proposition of a pragmatic citizen, who saw salvation in a consultation of the Delphic oracle, so justly renowned everywhere: a consultation for which opulent offerings were prepared, destined to preserve the Calydonians from the oracle's habitual embarrassing ambiguity. An ambassador was sent, and his return, awaited with impatience, in the disorderly assault of the sanctuaries, by the fraction of the people still spared, was favorable.

The prophetess had declared that the troublesome delirium by which the Calydonians were afflicted would cease its divagating and sometimes homicidal action when the young woman who had brought it on by her cruelty had ceased to soil the city with her presence. To liberate brains from such prejudicial vesanic vapors, it was necessary that Callirhoe be immolated to Bacchus by Coresos, his priest; however, the god would accept another victim if anyone, voluntarily, wanted to save the life of the condemned young woman and sacrifice their own for her.

Respectful of Pythic will, the envoys incited Callirhoe, if existence still seemed desirable and good to her, to seek someone who was willing to die in her place, and as the general interest could not suffer an unlimited wait, they signified to her that the dawn of the fourth day that followed would be her last daybreak.

Callirhoe made no response; disdainful of her probably inevitable death, she ignored it. Too proud to descend to supplications that might have saved her, she shut herself away in the gynaeceum, attentive to preserving her last hours from the afflicting contact of the indifferent. The ironic evil, in falling upon the ephebes, took away the rare chances of salvation that she might have had in precious vanities. No one among the young, ordinarily ardent for meritorious and long-praised devotions, could now perceive the attractive grandeur of a sacrifice that would have been recompensed in the future by the grateful cult of numerous generations. Folly had taken away all pride, and even dubious pity lay in the depths of few souls. Callirhoe was condemned, and, the three long days having passed, the morning rose that was to be fatal for her.

Coresos awaited it impatiently. He had reduced myrrh and cinnamon to smoke before the Master mitered in gold to whom he owed that supreme joy. He had dreamed about that white cleavage, scarcely glimpsed in previous encounters, into which he would soon plunge an amorously cruel knife. His passion, still alive in the midst of his anger, caused the moment when his sacerdotal tenderness would ravish Calirrhoe from the future amour that he had always dreaded desperately seem sweet to him. No one, thus, would possess the woman by whom he had been misjudged.

III

The cortège penetrated into the temple, in the middle of a joyful crowd, exhilarated by the hope of an imminent liberation, and voices—not cruel, certainly, merely impatient—howled frenetic abuse at Coresos, who was waiting by the altar with the tragic pallor of the oblation.

When he perceived Callirhoe, clad in white and crowned with hyacinths, he felt his murderous resolution weakening, and addressed the audience abruptly, asking in a tremulous voice: "Is there none among you who is willing to die for Callirhoe?"

Callirhoe looked at him haughtily.

"By what right," she said, "do you ask that question, which I did not want to emerge from your mouth? Under the vain pretext of a scorn once expressed, and what you perhaps believe to be a bond, do you think to extract a final consent from me? Cease then, sacrificer, to implore a devotion that I disdain; your god is waiting, and these men also."

Approving exclamations welcomed Callirhoe's words, and murmurs reaching the priest's ears made him understand how inopportune his intervention seemed. At the young woman's insult, however, he had relived the forgotten minutes. In evoking the former rigors, Callirhoe caused the affection that her refusals had wounded, but not killed, to be reborn, and the despair of losing his lover gripped Coresos, who straightened up and talked wildly to the people, who thought him mad:

"O Calydonians, whose ancestors were valorous in battles, devotees of the immortals who rendered destinies propitious, how cowardly you have become! If no one is found disposed to the pitiful heroism of redeeming a virgin, divine among virgins, what will become of the city in days of grim war, when it is necessary to come back on or under shields? Old men of Calydon, it will be written in your history that courage was dead in the city and that the fear of death, even religious and superb, haunted your darkened minds. In spite of you, however, Callirhoe shall not die."

Desperate clamors were heard. The invalids whom a residue of reason still illuminated, appealed for the expiatory immolation that would deliver them, and the healthy, terrified by the idea of menacing calamities, ran with arms extended toward the young woman, whom they wanted to seize and perhaps to slaughter. But Coresos cried: "Stop!"

His voice was so terrible that they all recoiled, and the pontiff addressed his god.

"Bacchus, royal conqueror whose quadrigas were drawn by gentled lions and tender panthers, forgive me if I forsake you, but Eros is stronger. You granted my prayers, I shall satisfy your order. Here is the victim you desired!"

He spoke, and, raising the knife, he struck himself with a firm hand; then, murmuring the name of Callirhoe, he slid down the steps of the bloody altar, and came to expire at the feet of the woman who had been fatal for him.

The Image

To E. Bernard.[1]

A little of that water, our mirrors.
Henri de Régnier.

HAVING wandered all day over the slopes of Helicon dear to the Pierides, the tired hunters descended into the valley watered by the Lamos, and near Hedonacon, where the reeds were quivering, they found the goatherd Thespis.

"Herdsman," they said, "we are weary. Our feet are wounded by the thorny gorse of the mountains; the spiteful jujube-trees have pierced our arms and labored our faces, and the city to which we are going is still far away."

"Hunters," Thespis replied, "dusk is falling; look, it is clothing the meadows with a mantle of hyacinth. Soon, the black coursers will be prancing on the horizon; Empusa, shaking the ground with her brazen slippers, will lead you astray in the paths that border the river and maliciously cause you to perish. Stay with Thespis until dawn. There, in that clump of odorous lentisks, is a spring surrounded

---

1 Lazare's younger brother Edmond, born in 1868.

jealously by bearded elms. On its banks, softened by pennyroyal and fern, you will find white hides, soft and gentle to fatigued men. For you, the milk will spring forth crowned with foam in clay jars, you will eat piquant cheese dried over woodchips, russet figs and honey that a Sybarite would appreciate."

"We would like that, Thespis, for our water-skins are flaccid and our food-bags empty. A quarter of venison will complete the offered repast, and when we have eaten, you can recount to us, accompanying yourself on the pipes dear to herdsmen, an adventure of gods or heroes."

And, the meat having been cooked over a fire of vine-branches, they lay down on the candid fleeces and sated themselves in silence, for they were very hungry. Afterwards, they begged the welcoming herdsman again, and Thespis, with benevolence, took up his flute and pronounced a prelude:

"O Pan, who strike with your goat's feet the summit of the high Menalos, now that dusk has darkened the meadows and the hills, permit the beloved sound of the Syrinx to reverberate. The vibrant airs of the reed please you, Pan, when, rested from your fatigues, you get up in the midst of the bushy woods."

The rustic sound, of a tender harmony, awoke the thickets and the bushes, and the footfalls of Hyleores stirred the clearings.

The god having been evoked, the goatherd commenced:

"Listen, hunters, to the morose adventure of the unfortunate son of Liriope, and when you have heard it, you will repeat with the Megaran Theognis: 'Of all goods, the most desirable for the inhabitants of the earth is not to be born."[1]

"You, Polupous, watch the herd."

With a vigorous bark, the mastiff testified its zeal, but Thespis imposed silence on it and he said:

"Narcissus, divine ephebe, Narcissus, it is of you that I want to sing. The day on which Cephissus of the foamy beard who is adored at Orope engendered you, he engendered the most beautiful of young men. Narcissus, O Narcissus!

"Your stature was similar to the bearing of poplars, your limbs had the suppleness of pink ivy, your hair was as blond as honey and your cheeks as gilded as helichrysum. As Dionyus advances in the midst of Olympians, so you marched among men. Maidens blushed under your gaze, for in their souls the sight of you stimulated amorous desires, and some, the boldest, went to spy on you at the edge of springs, Potamides coveting an adolescent god.

"No woman ever saw you, Narcissus, without desiring you, but perhaps, in the dormant wood, you were caressed by the huntress goddess, by Artemis of the slender legs, who roams the embalmed Syrtis populated with baying packs. Doubtless she chose you, as Endymion was once chosen, and from that day on you rejected the wishes of mortals, and even the amour of nymphs.

"How many cherished you! How many, alas, you rendered lamentable and desolate! Echo, who proclaimed her

---

1 Theognis of Megara, who lived in the sixth century B.C. did indeed include this remark in one of his poems, but probably did not originate it; several of the other sources quoting the complete aphorism (which adds "and after that, to die young") attribute it to Silenus, the faun-like associate of Bacchus, who was captured by humans and tortured to make him release the secret of human life.

fury to rocks saddened by the blackness of moss; Echo, whose imprecations are repeated by lairs and solitary vales; Echo, whose insensible lover you were! Aminias, more vindictive, who summoned upon you the vengeance of Aphrodite, and others too: the weeping cortege of widows who had never been spouses, moaning doves bearing their plaint to the bushy thickets, and beside the Lamos with the lulling waves that send the desperate to sleep.

"But one cannot laugh with impunity at the cruel master of the world, the omnipotent god under whom the gods tremble, and those who scorn him are punished, sooner or later. Did you not know, son of the river, the destinies of Hippolytus born of Theseus, and did your nurse, while cradling you on her knees, not murmur his story to you? Like him, you were struck, Narcissus, and by the hand of magiciennes, Cypris had you drink from the cup covered by the crimson fleece of a lamb.

"How beautiful the evening was, and yet it became bleak when you encountered, near the spring, the one who was victorious, and who ought not to have been. Certainly, Zeus espoused majestic Hera, whom a same womb had carried, but the actions of gods are not penetrable by men, and it does not befit us to act like them. As Oedipus and Hippodamia were criminal, so Narcissus was criminal.[1]

"You, over whom the most desirable were unable to triumph, were to be conquered by the one for whom you could only know a fraternal amity.

"Liriope had conceived her on the night that you were conceived, and the morning that saw you born heard her

---

1 The version of the story of Narcissus in which he falls in love with his twin sister is unique, in ancient sources, to Pausanias, in the same text from which Lazare appropriated the story of Coresos and Callirhoe.

wail too. She was your equal in beauty, your equal in grace; you were like two twin stars, and no one could tell you apart, for her stature was similar to the bearing of poplars, her limbs had the suppleness of pink ivy, her hair was as blonde as honey and her cheeks as gilded as helichrysum. She waked among her companions as Hebe advances in the midst of the immortals. Her charm seduced the ephebes, and some went to spy on her at the outflow of lakes, lascivious aegipans lying in wait for an Elionome.

"In the depths of the gynaeceum, guardian of virgins, in the shade of flowery clumps of bloody pomegranates, under the vines stirred by the shrill flight of bees, in the forests and on the river banks, everywhere you voiced your amour, from the day when, by way of the hands of magiciennes, Cypris had you drink from the cup covered with the crimson fleece of a lamb.

"Wildly, she fled from you, and did not respond to your husbandly kisses by any caress, even sisterly. She had a horror of your desires, and her hands repelled your embrace when, madly, you wanted to seize her in the solitude of the woods.

"And your heart melted, and you shed the tears of dolor, and you knew henceforth the anguishing tortures that your lovers had known; you understood the heartbreak of Echo, the anger of Aminias; your eyes were covered by a veil of sad tears.

"More painful still for you were the chagrins. You could not tell anyone about them, and a man is unfortunate who cannot relate his torments. The sage has said that humans love to confide their joys to their fellows, for they sharpen them by the possible anger of the confidant, but the desolate individual believes that his tearful pain will awaken obscure tremors of sympathy in the souls of his brethren.

"Destiny, however, reserved bitter and new tortures for you, Narcissus, deplorable Narcissus! One summer evening, in the time when the air palpitates with a frisson of wings, when the woods are stirred by birdsong, when the meadows quiver with perfumed vibrations, she died, the sweet virgin; bleak and sad, she died of the despair of your amour. She was laid on the bed of scabious, the customary libations were made, and people groaned: 'Pale corpse, for you Eros did not sneeze. . . .'

"Of what solitudes did you demand your sister and your lover, unfortunate ephebe! With what cries did you appeal to her! With what supplications did you importune the gods who were punishing you! And the bitterness of your regrets was so great that all of them felt pity, even Queen Aphrodite.

"She heard your dolorous clamors, the benevolent Anadyomene, the dispenser of cherished joys. Her soul was moved; she wanted to console you, to calm your distress, to render the light of the sun supportable to you. She was close to you, doubtless, when, on the edge of the spring where the reeds were swaying, you attested your evil, which the Hedonaconian Creneas shared.[1] She curbed your face toward the calm waters, and you saw yourself reflected there, O Narcissus!

"Is it really your image, sad widower, that the obliging waters are sending back to you. No, for those features you saw once in the disappeared lover. You uttered a great cry, and the Orodemniades of the mountains heard it in

______

1 Creneas [Crénées] in the original, like several of the other exotic terms in the story (Hyleores, Elionomes, Potamides and Orodemniades), is an exotic term referring to a type of nymph.

the distance, surprised and frightened. Then you leaned over, kneeling on the fresh balm, and your lips touched the humid surface, which returned your kiss. It was really her, the Virgin who had not espoused you; she lived again in the mirror of the benevolent waters, and your heart was appeased and your senses calmed.

"She was not irredeemably lost, the Adored One, and Thanatos had returned her less cruel, since she suffered your caresses without the habitual wrath.

"From then on you abandoned Thespia and the house that solemnized the hearth, and you lived beside Hedonacon. You spoke with the rediscovered one and listened to her responses in the plash of wavelets, in the murmur of mosses steaming with dew. For you the dawns and the noons, the dusks and the lunar nights, seemed like rare and ever-new gems, and alone you possessed her, in the propitious silence created by the great oaks.

"One day, you wanted her entirely, her smile alone was no longer sufficient, and the water opened, which was not nuptial, and you went to sleep without the beloved, for the gods, irritated by your untiring covetousness, withdrew her from your desire.

"Narcissus, unfortunate Narcissus, the Moirai have been rigorous for you; you never saw a fortunate morning shine. And you repeat again, with the exceedingly wise Megaran: 'Of all goods, the most desirable for the inhabitants of the earth is not to be born.'"

As Thespis had sung well, the hunters offered him a rustic cup that a skillful artist had carved in wood. Then they all went to sleep, while Polupous watched the vagabond goats.

Death Renounced

To Léon Dierx.[1]

I shall reveal to you what you tried to seize.
G. Flaubert.[2]

I

AS the crowd around him had grown, the man who was meditating, sitting on the steps of the Paneum, had risen to his feet. He leaned on the balustrade and silently contemplated Alexandria, which embraced the artificial hill on all sides. The sun, facing him, broke its rays on the shiny waves on which foam put a diaphanous fringe of lace, and the sea varied the blue of its ripples endlessly. It splashed somber patches above the rocks and then brightened in harmonious degradations that placed, alongside intense cobalts, the calmest lapis and translucent sapphires, while the horizon was tinted by a placidly bluish

---

1 Léon Dierx (1838–1912) was an associate of Leconte de Lisle and Mallarmé and a significant Parnassian poet, much admired by the younger generation of Symbolist poets.
2 The quotation presumably comes from Flaubert's *Salammbô* (1862), referring to the veil of Tanit.

gray, confounded with the sky, which was only separated from the waves by a violet-tinted line.

On the isle of the Pharos, where the houses of mariners were huddled around the beacon, the sunlight attained the white tower, so the marble was rose-tinted here and there, slightly, like the skin of a virgin unveiled. Then the city spread out, with its two immense avenues and its mysterious files of sphinxes, its houses with flat roofs and painted colonnettes, its pylons coiffed with winged disks, its temples, the porticos of its palaces, and its gardens of acacias and sycamores. The gilded cupola of the Serapeum dominated the southern quarters and enlarged the Brachium of the thousand edifices, among them the Soma, where Alexander was dreaming in his golden coffin. To the left, Lake Mareotis was asleep; to the right, the freshly washed country, and in the distance the river furrowed by thalamegi, whose sails inflated in the wind.

The man gazed for a long time, and the silence was so great that, in the death of the city, made torpid by the hour, the discreet sound of tambourines was heard, cheering up the barges descending toward Canope.

However, the dreamer awoke, with a slight shrug of the shoulders, perhaps in order to abolish tangible visions within him, and only then did he see those who were doubtless waiting for him to speak. They were multiple in aspect, races and attitudes; there were negroes whose uncertain pupils seemed to be dreaming of regretted landscapes traversed by the heavy tread of elephants; there were pale Greeks with a trailing gait, Gauls and Dacians, Arabs and Cimmerians, and Jews, whose temple sheltered under its vestibule the steles of foreign kings. The mixture of castes was no less great: slaves with backs polluted by the calluses of whips, brushed with their rags the litters in which courtesans laid back on cushions, heads rendered heavy by excessively ornamented hair; soldiers helmed in bronze; embalmers from the Necropolis and fellahs from Rakotis bumped into scribes and merchants come from Tyre; priests of Osiris brushed with their animal skins the linen robes of Hierosolymitani exegetes.

In spite of those apparent disharmonies, a hidden bond appeared to unite the crowd; a mysterious affinity attached such various individuals to one another. In their hollow eyes, which appeared to be searching in souls for the same and constant thought, the secret of their fraternity was legible, for those eyes recounted a bleak and similar ennui, an equal anguish, like special mirrors that would have revealed the intimate and unexpected similarity of different visages.

And the contemplative silence of the man was prolonged, and exaggerated the mute impatience of the crowd, attentive to the glimpsed gestures that would be the precursors of speech. Suddenly, however, from the bed on which she lay, a woman sat up and, extending with difficulty her arm laden with golden rings and chains, she abused the man who was not speaking.

"Hegesias,"[1] she said, "do not augment my desires. Long has been the journey during which I felt them increase, and I have waited too long. To see you, to hear you,

---

1 Hegesias of Cyrene, who lived toward the end of the third century B.C., was a pessimistic philosopher who argued that happiness is impossible to achieve, but there is no evidence to support the claim made by Cicero that he wrote a book called *Death by Starvation*, which prompted so many suicides that he was nicknamed Peisithanatos [death-persuader] and banned from teaching in Alexandria. Lazare extrapolates that anecdote considerably.

I quit Antioch, the city where darkness is unknown. I have left my palace populated with women and slaves ready to serve my will, the gardens of Daphne, flourishing with laurels, embalmed by privet and myrtle, and the covered porticos between which my chariots circulated.

"I am twenty years old, Hegesias, and no joy is tempting for me; in vain you would seek to offer me a pleasure that I have not rejected scornfully; for a long time I have been weary. My flesh has quivered at all the kisses and even the memory is not within me, of the most chaste as of the most impure; no transport, subtle or ingenious, ever awakens the ice of my body. I have summoned actors from Berytus, dancers from Caesaria, musicians from Gaza, but none has been able to break the sigillary ennui of my soul; no one, neither the wrestlers of Ascalon nor the pugilists of Castabala. In feasts, when the precious wines flow, when unknown venisons render the guests open-mouthed, the odor of the perfumes of Babylon changes for me into an acrid smoke; the songs of harpists, the words of rhetors and the verses of poets sound in my ear like the vain echo of a vain din, and the lascivious gestures of flute-players leave my too-oft-violated senses asleep. My mind is weary, even of dreams, which, for some time, have been my puerile stimulations, and the unexpected has fled, for everything awakes in my being obscure and familiar vibrations.

"One day, someone spoke to me of you; someone who had seen you in Syracuse told me that you knew persuasive words, healing words, and that you knew the liberating remedy for our deprived hearts. I have come without believing it, and since this morning, when I entered the city, I have followed the crowd that led me to you. But now, careless of impatience, you stay silent. Speak, then, if your benevolent voice is going to render the next dawn new to me, and the next kiss desirable."

Exhausted, her voice weary, she let herself fall back into the depths of her litter, and as, in spite of her supplications, the silence persisted, an old man crouching in the dust stood up.

"Although," he said, "the evocative appeal of that woman has been unable to touch you, perhaps you will hear me, Hegesias. Have no fear of tedious speeches from me, my discourse will be brief. If the rumor of your glory is not deceptive, you ought to know, instructed by secret ways, what no one has yet been able to tell me. Many, it is said, come to you anxious who quit you satisfied with things said, glad of the future finally unveiled. You, who liberate anguish, reveal to an old man whose soul is worn out the soporific doctrine of which he has come to you in quest, as a disciple."

Then, in a soothing voice with slow cadences, Hegesias spoke, with calm gestures that seemed to be dressing wounds.

"In the mystery of a clear statement, uncomprehended by virtue of its very clarity, the truth is hidden. Those who die young are beloved by the gods, the sage has pronounced, and so limpid is the formula that men repeat it without suspecting its latent value; for it is true that the thickest veil is the one that gives the illusion of light. Simplicity is so disconcerting that one can bury the absolute within it with impunity; thus an essential aphorism becomes banal. If the benevolence of the gods is manifest in Death finally granted, is it not the case that Death is the sovereign good?

"Some have understood that primary significance of the axiom, but that is not sufficient; they dare not draw the conclusion from the premises posited. Ought they not, however, to conceive, after the revelation made of the supreme joy, how licit and praiseworthy its voluntary research becomes? In a word, ought they not to arrive at the definitive vision that, Death being the glorious goal of life, it is important for them to go toward the liberation from such disastrous brief hours?

"Certainly, doubtless many a time, the ineffable voluptuousness of tombs has invaded your hearts. On sad evenings, when dolor weeps within you; on cheerful mornings, when the radiant sun renders even more poignant the memory of dear presences disappeared, you have felt—have you not?—a morose and gentle breath brushing your flesh, as a nocturnal wind strips the petals from crepuscular flowers over still lakes. Alas, that instant when, truly wise, you summoned Death, was fleeting, for the desire for good peace stimulated for you all the atavistic and age-old terrors. So I have come to say to you: chase away vain fears; enable yourselves to escape freely.

"From existence comes evil—not only transitory evil but eternal evil, and it is by virtue of ancient and deeply rooted opinions that you place your ends in the mutable universe. Gripped by the irresistible fear of infinity, you never cease to hide from eternal things, and each of your minutes flees from them madly. All action is soiling: if it is vile, in itself; if it is good, by the regret it leaves of wishes never realized. Thus, in acting, you wrap your soul in deplorable bonds, and its survival is no longer what it ought to be, the ascension toward its essence, but the return to terrestrial peregrinations.

"Set aside the malign occasions, the tempting passions, say the philosophers. Do they not know that the world perpetually extends traps in which to capture the flesh, and no one is able to avoid them, for we are all flesh. The spirit, the prisoner king, cannot triumph over matter, and Death alone can break that dolorous duality. Leave, then, the ignorant and the weak to await the belated and assigned hour, and come to Death. She is welcoming and gentle; she is the guardian of stellar gardens, the hierophant of infallible joys; she liberates and creates, she is the victor of sly ambushes, the dispensatrice of true life. Old men detached from doctrines, women disappointed by enjoyments, young men already weary, abandon your stained bodies, putrescence and forgetfulness will be sweet to them after the sufferings undergone; hasten toward the real delights, give yourselves fearlessly to maternal Death."

Hegesias fell silent; he leaned on the balustrade again and, pensively, his gaze wandered over the waters. The sun was declining, the marble tower loomed up, pale and as if saddened by ardent kisses fled too soon; the sea appeased its flamboyance, its waves swelled; it commenced the sob of the quotidian dusk, the eternal plaint, ever repeated, of the female lover forsaken by the wild male lover. In the orient, tenuous mists veiled the sky, pale vapors rose from the weary earth, and on the river, light gauzes trailed.

The streets of the city were populated by a noisy and busy crowd; the harbor resounded with a tumult of voices; naked negroes were unloading vessels filled with wheat, whose grain fell back in dull and dusty cascades, and merchants hastened, jostling the slaves. The flat roofs of the houses were strewn with cushions and fabrics; women lay upon them lazily; they were gazing at the Nile, where the little sails of boats were quivering, and listening to the sounds of flutes that resounded more forcefully in the brothels of Eleusis. Here and there, on belvederes, sacred ibises sat, immobile and melancholy.

Those who surrounded the man had drawn closer. Some were speaking to him with gestures of invocation; the woman from Antioch lowered the flaps of her mantle, and the old man who had spoken prostrated himself. Those whose minds had not grasped the word and those who had been frightened by it fled; others, on the contrary, precipitated themselves from the top of the hill, struck themselves with their daggers or strangled themselves with the girdles of their robes. Many, modestly, perhaps disdainful of a death that would be exemplary, hastened toward the solitude where good Death was waiting for them; and the irresolute, their faces haggard, irrevocably troubled by the things said, sat down on the steps like supplicants on the steps of a temple.

Hegesias harangued them again:

"Insensates, how precious existence must appear to you, since you still desire it after the revelation made of its pernicious inanity. Do you believe, then, that I have spoken in vain? Do you not sense that the mere memory of my speech will render detestable to you the most desired pleasures, for the truth is such that even those contemptuous of it are dominated by it? Come to me! Soon I shall not be able to convince you. The hour is near when my voice will cease to resound in the gardens and under the porticos; listen to my supreme exhortations; they will give you well-being and peace. If not, the proffered syllables, which will never die away entirely, will resonate for a long time in your hearts, and what was a salutary balm for the disciples will be a bitter bile for you."

Abruptly, he stopped speaking. He had heard the foot-falls of cohorts shaking the steps of the Paneum, and, hoplites armed with pikes having invaded the platform, he marched toward them, pushing aside the faithful who clung to his garments.

"Let go," he said. "You have no more need of me; I have given you the Word."

A scribe who was accompanying the soldiers advanced, unrolled a parchment, and read:

"Since, in spite of reiterated advice, and even orders, the philosopher Hegesias continues publicly to spread his doctrines, harmful to the State, which he deprives of necessary citizens; since benevolent injunctions no longer appear to have sufficient authority and he persists, doubt-less motivated by a desire for banal glory, to pervert young people with a captious eloquence, it is good and just that Hegesias, called Peisithanatos by his disciples, be retained in the prisons of the city, until the day when it pleases Ptolemy, our king, to render the justice that cannot fail."

Hegesias shrugged his shoulders, and descended the marble staircase silently.

II

Early that morning the gardens of the tribunal were populated by a crowd, simultaneously hostile, friendly or indifferently curious, come to see Hegesias summoned. The speech of enemy rhetors resounded, criticizing with a bitterness tempered by a malevolent joy the discourse of the accused philosopher, and from the group of disciples, no protest rose up, but only regrets and plaints.

As soon as the doors opened, the hall of justice was invaded, and the silence was very great when Hegesias entered and came to place himself before the Archidicaste, who was surrounded by judges and scribes, and protected by the royal guards.

An exegete sustained the accusation that the most important men of all the demes had launched elsewhere.

"In the name of the King," he declared, "in the name of the venerable and sage elders, I accuse Hegesias Peisithanatos, self-styled philosopher, of corrupting the young and inciting them to actions, or rather an action, prejudicial to themselves and to the city."

"What have you to respond, Hegesias?" asked the Archidicaste.

"Too much," relied the philosopher, "but I shall be brief. I am accused of having excited the ephebes of the city to harmful determinations. So be it, but then, O most enlightened judges, it would be necessary to prove to me that life is a desirable good and that Death, whose research I recommend, an incontestable evil. You are not mad enough, old man, to sustain that existence in Elysian dwellings is less enviable than our customary vagabondage in this world, prey to dolor. You would not dare, would you, to accuse of lying the glorious poets and sages who have professed that opinion at all times? Perhaps in your youth, you even composed an epitaph for the tomb of a friend prematurely struck down, in which you envied him strolling through the fields of asphodel in the company of Homer and Orpheus. If you are sincere, as I am, you will admit that to me, and you will doubtless no longer consider it extraordinary that, thinking thus, I have taught its incontestable verity. If that is the case, my crime is, I believe, in the eyes of my most active enemies, that of having been able to persuade by my doctrine, while so many Alexandrian sophists speak in vain for theirs."

A few rumors rose up in the auditorium. Without paying any heed to them, Hegesias continued:

"As for the prejudice caused to the city, I have never preoccupied myself with that. All action appearing indifferent to me, save for the definitive and liberating act, I do not think about the positive value of gestures, and I have certainly deprived that State, by my counsels, of soldiers, rhetors and perhaps even judges. I do not repent of that. Also, careless of monetary considerations, it is probable that I have offended fiscal rights in depriving Alexandria of productive citizens. I cannot, while confessing my fault, offer my wealth in compensation; having always lived in austerity and abstinence, I possess nothing.

"Furthermore, if you demand it, benevolent judges, I will say that the example was pernicious of a man scorning the busy occupations of his fellows; knowing the vanity of those temporary concerns, knowing that each of my terrestrial hours was stolen from eternity, my mind could not be tempted by any of your ambitions. Thus, I admit having perverted the young, but, unlike you, I mean those that I have not informed. Now, if it is necessary to condemn me for that infraction of hypothetical duties, I will say, like Socrates: 'Inflict a fine on me; my friends, in default of myself, will be able to pay it.'"

Hegesias having fallen silent, the Archidicaste reflected for a moment, and said to him: "Do you not believe, Hegesias, that it is a despicable sophist who does not conform his actions scrupulously to his words?"

"I believe it, as I have never esteemed the insensate glorifying wisdom, nor the debauchee magnifying continence."

"Then, if you are convinced that it is necessary to perish in order to flee suffering; if Thanatos, redoubtable to mortals, appears to you to be the sole god worthy of an effective worship, why do you content yourself with recommending death to your disciples? The example of your voluntary demise would, however, be profitable to them. When the powerful Alexander traveled the lands that Bacchus had once traversed triumphantly, the gymnosophist Kalanos, desirous of proving his scorn for life, burned himself ecstatically before the army. Why have you not done likewise?"

"In asking me that question," the philosopher replied, "you show clearly that it would be impossible for you to understand the reason for my conduct. In spite of that, I shall reply to you, not for you, and not for those who surround you; I am speaking only to those believers who might have been troubled by your insidious question.

"When, after having suffered, after having searched for a long time, I recognized that dolor came through all our senses open to the noise of the illusory universe; when I had understood that the sole remedy was to close them forever, certainly, I ought not to have had any other desire than that of realizing the emergent vision. But, like you, magistrate, like you, old men of the demes, I was concerned for the fate of my fellows, and the pity that some of them inspired in me, although less practical, equaled yours. I had listened to them groaning so often, heard them imploring supreme consolations so many times, that my heart resounded henceforth with all their plaints, and each of their sobs bruised me.

"And, knowing the words that would be sweet and saving, having the power to dry up their tears, to cure their pustules and their wounds, and open the sidereal dwellings to them where happiness resides, I should kill myself? Like the miser, the hoarder of jewels and gems, I should have guarded jealously the good news and been inattentive to their woes? Men, you recompense with unusual honors those who have made to the city or those whom they cherish the sacrifice of their life; that is just, for those heroes attached a high price to the goods renounced. But I, for whom existence is a lamentable burden, for whom death is the desired end, the dearest dream, have made to those I love the sacrifice of my death.

"I have said everything. What can you do against me? Condemn me to death? Accompanied by the rudest tortures, the end would still be welcome to me; and if you let me live, you will not be imposing anything on me that I have not already chosen."

For a long time the judges conferred in low voices, in hesitant perplexity; then, the oldest among them having pronounced a few words, they suddenly became serene, and the Archidicaste, having risen to his feet, pronounced the sentence.

"Hegesias, the equitable tribunal, in the name of Ptolemy, condemns you to live . . . to live alone."

The Lyre

To J.-M. de Heredia.[1]

I
Neanthes

Look! I have the rhythm and the divine contour.
Léon Dierx.

IT was in the gardens of Daphne, where the laurier-roses are interlaced with cypresses, mingling their bright corollas with the somber foliage of the tree dear to Aphrodite; in the gardens of Daphne, where the fresh voice resounds of a thousand springs born in the depths of grottos, and the waters of which spread out among the melancholy asphodels of the meadows.

Archytas the merchant, in order to celebrate the fifth lustrum of his public functions, had gathered his friends in his villa and, in the banqueting hall, lying on tortoise-

---

1 José-Maria de Heredia (1842–1905) was born in Cuba, but educated in France, where he subsequently settled, becoming—in spite of his meager production and negligible publication—an important member of the Parnassian Movement, closely associated with Charles Leconte de Lisle. His salon became an important hub of the Symbolist Movement in the late 1880s.

shell beds, the guests were amusing themselves with the gestures of mimes and the leaps of ballerinas. There was Hermogenes, son of Charmidas, Menippus the Satirist; Cresphontes of Gaza, the physician Aretas, Casus Pius, the illustrious rhetor, and the poets Euphorion and Philodemus of Gadara.[1]

Wreathed with roses and hyacinths, anointed with precious balms, they celebrated the delicacy of the dishes offered, and, while powdered children chosen from among the most beautiful allowed the bloody pearls of wines issued from distant countries to fall, drop by drop, from perforated rhytons, they praised the generosity of their host. The odor of turpentine, with which the wineskins were perfumed, mingled with the insidious clouds of myrrh fuming in golden braziers, and the crepitation of water jets falling back on marble was audible in spite of the flute that an ambubaia was playing.

Meanwhile, the slaves had just removed the seventh course, and the merchant's guests, lying back on the silver-draped periclinia, were following with dreaming eye the lascivious undulations of dancers whose cleavages were darkened by a wad of perfumes, when Castus Pius, the rhetor, who was having his patera filled with water by a curly-haired adolescent, made a gesture that demanded silence. At a sign from Archytas, the dances ceased and the harmonies fell silent.

---

1 Although these characters are probably all fictitious, their names are borrowed from characters in Greek history or mythology. Aretus might be intended to be the celebrated physician Aretaeus, who lived in the first century A.D., but he was not contemporary with the poet Euphorion of Chalcis, who lived in the third century B.C. The latter was approximately contemporary with the satirist Menippus of Gadara, but not the philosopher and poet Philodemus of Gadara, who lived in the first century B.C.

"Do you not think," said Castus Pius, "that we could justly be said to be as gluttonous as coots if, at Archytas' feast, we contented ourselves with the temporary satisfaction that the intoxication of wines and the charms of dishes produces?"

"Although there is a lot to be said for the pleasure you scorn, Pius, your words are nevertheless judicious," replied the physician Aretas, "but I would like you to make your thought more precise, and none of us will complain about that, for you are the subtlest of the subtle."

"The wine of Ptelea, which you appear to be drinking, Aretas, must have clouded your brain," replied Menippus. "If you do not penetrate the aphorisms of the venerable Hippocrates better than you have grasped Pius' desire, your patients must complain of your art."

"Your wit is facile," said Aretas, "but those who understand the arguments of Isocrates have them developed in order to increase their joy."

"You know how to flatter, Aretas, and flattery is so sweet, even for the blasé, that you oblige me to speak," riposted Castus Pius. "At the banquet that was made illustrious by the divine Socrates, did not Alcibiades send away the saltatrices in order to permit the guests to speak freely about Eros and Anteros? The example is a good one to follow, and I see enough savant minds around me for the pleasure of their discourse to substitute for the incitement of attitudes and mimics, which is, after all, facile."

"Would you like to make a dissertation on amour?" asked Hermogenes.

"Socrates said it all," observed Cresphonte.

"One has never said it all," remarked Castus Pius, "and even Aretas would be able to find a new definition."

"And you?" queried Aretas.

"I could, perhaps, find several."

"Does amour interest you to the point of forming the unique object of your discussions?" asked Euphorion.

"Doubtless the others think that it's the only subject worthy of a few men who have drunk and eaten amply," said Philodemus.

"Propose another theme to us," Menippus insinuated.

"And which is more beautiful than poetry," said Euphorion and Philodemus,

"Why not medicine?" protested Aretas.

"Because few of us could follow you, Aretas, and we could all participate in the Art of Arts, eternal poetry."

"Well said, Pius. You know that the attractions of Homer are more universal than those of Galen and Celsius," said Cresphontes.

"Yes, for a physician is a more or less skillful artisan, and the poet is the immortal king of men, the equal of the jealous gods," said Philodemus.

"Why jealous?" interrogated Hermogenes.

"Because they don't permit their voices to be borrowed, and wish misfortune upon those who want to steal the lyre," proffered Euphorion.

"Those who want to take it for evil purposes."

"Also those who seize it with a view to good, O Pius," proclaimed Philodemus.

"Explain yourself, Philodemus."

"I don't know how to discourse in accordance with the rules, Pius; the laws of sophism are unknown to me. It's necessary that I dress my thoughts in the pompous mantle of images, and that I enclose them in myths, sometimes as obscure as nights prey to mystery, sometimes as clear as summer dawns."

"Sing, then, Philodemus; none of us, certainly, will be annoyed by that."

"Let it be as you desire."

And, supporting his elbow momentarily on his tortoiseshell bed, Philodemus meditated; then, in a vibrant voice, he spoke thus:

"In the darkness of Thrace, the river had quivered, the river whose waves echo the clamors of the Mimallones who howled on the mountains in the darkness of Thrace.

"The waves have quivered to bear the divine head that lies on your neglected Lyre, like a dead man in the arms of his lover, the eternal lover who must survive despair and go in quest of other lovers. Oh, Hebrus in mourning, Hebrus whose mirror reflected the torches of the Bacchantes and the thunderbolt of the furious god; Hebrus in mourning, whose reeds palpitated to the breath of the violet mouth that the Lyre presents to the skies.

"Mouth still living in spite of the cruel death, the river stops in listening to your plaint, and slowly, for the waters, captive of proffered songs, retain it, the glorious head advances toward the sea, which hears it and will soon quiver to bear it.

"And the journey is slow also, the journey over the seductive seas, the seas whose profound swell falls silent before the dolor of the widowed Lyre and the head still infatuated with the poems that it engenders and speaks: a slow and bleakly sad voyage, which the marine goddesses accompany, pitiful virgins wiping the melancholy eyes of Orpheus with their hair; a mournful cortege that rides the wave wreathed with pearls and florid with unknown diamonds, which unfurl over the flanks of the Lyre and are confounded with its tears.

"The Ocean around you laments; it sheds the immemorial gems of its tears, and the glaucous mantle of the Nereids is paled by their placid gleam. The old Ocean remembers the insensible Argo that your fascinating voice caused to march, husband of Eurydice, whom Hades wanted to keep.

"The shore is perceived of the isle of sad sensualities, Lesbos, crowned with myrtles, and the Tritons put their conches ornamented with soft green algae to their lips. The conches, mute until then, resound to announce your advent, Aede victorious over the dragon. Lugubrious conches, again the echoes of Lesbos are stirred; they cast your voice into space, and the memory of the rocks awakens, reviving the fabulous morning that Orpheus saw.

"A morose wind brushes the jasmines and the privet, a wild wind pillages the gardens dressed with new roses; a benevolent wind sows corollas on the beach, and pushes the mutilated calices on to the water, and the head progresses, sustained by the flowers.

"Everything falls silent on Lesbos. On the slopes of the hills the trees make gestures of silence; the trees with immortal verdure, propitious guardians of amorous embraces. No sigh takes flight from Lesbos; Echo, pensive, listens to the sobbing of the rock that opens for the head of royal Orpheus.

"Rock verdant with age-old mosses, you are reddened by the blood that stopped the waves of the Thracian river and the mists of the plaintive sea: blood as bright as rutilant gems, lustral blood of the Lyre, O blood, holocaust of Zeus, blood of Orpheus.

"The strings vibrate in the evening, and the evening meditates, and in the evening the ground moans, the ground where the blood weeps, the sad blood of Orpheus, whose mouth palpitates: regret for the rhythms of old, dolor for the strophes that fled when, in the shroud of nights florid with stars, the body of the Aede was thrown by the furious maidens, delirious Lysiennes[1] submissive to the thyrsus-baring god, the supreme Bacchant mitered in gold.

"Why have the marvelous sounds propagated by the dusk come to assail your abode, King of Lesbos?[2] The veiled Destinies have brought them close to your couch, son of Pittacus, audacious young man, and you hear them.

"You have heard them, the immutable sounds that Linus himself was unable to capture; the eternal sounds that escaped when the silver egg of the world broke; the sounds that only the great gesture of Orpheus tamed!

"King of Lesbos, Neanthes, you heard the sounds. Fatal, irresistible, they guided you to the shore, and the clamor of your cortege chased away the pale nymphs who were watching over the head: the head crowned with glorious lilies and frank roses; the head that had just kissed the occanic waves.

"You hastened in your chariot strewn with hyacinths, surrounded by ephebes in loose robes, and equivocal

---

1 Although this word does exist in French it does not appear to have a meaning that makes sense in the present context; as s and d are adjacent on a typewriter keyboard it is possible that it is a typo and that Lazare intended to imply that the bacchantes in question were from Lydia.

2 The familiar version of the story of Neanthes' encounter with the lyre of Orpheus, in Ovid's *Metamorphoses*, makes him the son of the tyrant Pittacus, not the island's king; the latter detail appears to be an improvisation by Lazare.

maidens whose glaucous eyes were illuminated by perverse gleams. The axles of the chariot screeched plaintively on the strand, the wheels of the chariot sank into the sand with its soft undulations, and aegipans drunk on ripe grapes joined your insolent escort, O son of Pittacus.

"In the early morning air, your horses whinnied, their manes were alarmed, letting fall the ornamentation of garlands, when they saw the Lyre standing high on the rock; and your horses reared up before the Lyre, the Lyre that was weeping alone, forsaken on the edge of the maternal seas.

"Drunk on new breezes, the white stallions broke their reins; they fled toward the foam; they came face to face with the rock, and the mouth of Orpheus smiled sadly at their homages. The chariot that the white stallions had abandoned remained immobile.

"King Neanthes, you descended from your futile seat, and the plaits of your hair came undone as you marched. Your feet, your careless feet, collided with the whelks scattered on the beach; they caused to revive in their spirals the hymns of the marine plants, your feet, conducted by inflexible fate.

"The joyful pipes of satyrs led the chorus of young men, young guardians of the King. Amorous men and women, you danced your frivolous dances, and the soul of enamored Syrinx palpitated on the lips of the goatfoots, accomplices of your dances and your games. King Neanthes, you came, led by inflexible fate.

"You came toward the Destinies, and toward Death, and toward the Night, and you climbed the rocks, which agitated beneath your violating feet, the rocks that the blood of the hero had rendered sacred. Nothing stopped you in your sacrilege; neither the emotion of the stone nor the voice of the nymphs, nor the gaze of Orpheus. You held out your despoiling hands toward the divine Lyre, under the gaze of Orpheus.

"In order to conduct the procession of maidens and ephebes, you took the Lyre, King of Lesbos; the Lyre victorious over the Sirens; the Lyre that conceals the secrets of the Gods. Your unskillful fingers wandered over the strings, the astonished waves rushed to the horizons, the heavens were veiled, and tears gushed from the bewildered eyes of Orpheus.

"Your fingers have wakened the echoes of the dense woods, and what pack is baying on the flanks of the distant hills, pairs of dogs launched by the slopes of the bushy mountains? O vengeful pack! Here comes the Night, King Neanthes, here come Death and the Destinies.

"The hounds have overturned the chariot, they have dispersed the cortege; the aegipans have fled. The ivy and jasmine of crowns is mingled with the seashells of the shore; the rustic flutes of the satyrs strew the red sands. The unskillful fingers are no longer soiling the Lyre.

"It was terrible, your cry of agony, O son of Pittacus, audacious young man! You appealed to Orpheus, who turned his eyes away from you to contemplate the reconquered Lyre, and the cruel teeth of the dogs avenged the mocked gods; the dogs that are still howling in the plains; the plains of Lesbos, protectresses of Orpheus."

And Philodemus of Gadara leaned his elbow once again on the tortoiseshell bed, meditated again for a moment, and proffered, gravely: "Thus died Neanthes, for having touched the Lyre."

II
Marsyas

For the skin of the satyr is the plaything of the wind.
J.-M. de Heredia.

The poet had fallen silent, and in the room in which the fog of emanated incense was thickening, the guests, letting the roses on their foreheads shed their petals, were dreaming in an austere silence that the voice of Castus Pius broke.

"You have spoken well, Philodemus, and you have shown us the impiety chastised by the wrath of beneficent immortals. But were there not pious rhapsodists whose fate was enviable and mild?"

"Homer died blind and vagabond," murmured Philodemus.

"The hands of Maenads tore Orpheus apart," said Euphorion.

"Aeschylus was ridiculed by his sons," supplied Philodemus.

"Sappho saw the mouths of the sea extended toward her," added Euphorion.

"Are they the only aedes?" asked Castus Pius.

"Listen, rhetor," proclaimed Euphorion, "and you will know the jealousy of the gods."

And, getting up from the periclinium florid with corollas, he spoke thus:

"Olympus, may your name be dear to our memories, for you have buried the Satyr near Nysa, city of the Orgiaste, on the bank of the river of dolors.

"Tears of nymphs and tears of aegipans, blood of the flute-player, from you is born the river, the melancholy river of sobs. Tears, perpetual and morose tears, spring from the foot of the tree that buckles under the weight of the lacerated body, those who listen to you know the legend of the sad singer of Ida. Listen to the tears that are the waters.

"Oh naïve goat-foot, why did you not remain at peace, wandering over the flanks of the mountains, among the friendly flocks? The day, setting over the pennyroyal and the laburnum pursued you with the white cortege of your dreams and, at night, you slept in the soft bed made for you by the crimson fleece of ewes, Vagabond Marsyas, for whom destiny lay in wait.

"Ancestor of those who sing on the banks of gushing streams, the hour was misfortunate for you when you stole from the Tritonide guardian the accursed pipes that Athene forsook. The pipes were sleeping at the bottom of the clear lake; listen to the waters that are tears.

"Marsyas had stolen the imprisoned flute, and the soul of Marsyas is now the captive of the resuscitated sounds. His devotional fingers brush the holes of shadow and his lips unite with the lips of the pipes: the first kiss by which the valleys are stirred, the victimizing and sacred kiss. Listen to the tears, listen to the waters.

"On the rocks that protect the sleep of the waves, violated now, the Satyr is leaning. He has inflated his cheeks, he has inclined his head, the harmony has escaped and he stops, ecstatic. The waters weep that were your blood.

"Marsyas, you speak the joy of eyes, and the triumph of day. You speak the rustle of meadows, the song of lively springs, the proud hymn of the woods and the clamor of the mountains: haughty and touching voices, rude and fearful voices, you give birth to the appeal of the surprised singer, who perpetuates your rhythms and your cadences, and henceforth, you shall live the eternal life. Your blood weeps, O Satyr, your blood weeps in the waters.

"You have fled the tender arbors, and henceforth you wander as a vagabond, fugitive rhapsodist whom the goddess torments, to avenge her shame and her ugliness, at which the gods have laughed. To celebrate Pan, who palpitates in the most obscure blades of grass, is insufficient for your desires; you have encountered the Phrygienne; your softened heart is smitten with amour. The docile flute murmurs the glory of Cybele, the child of Dindymene, who has nursed the beasts and the woods. Lover, you have encountered the Phrygienne.

"Sweetness of confessions, mystery of kisses, emotion of exhaled plaints, the one to whom you submit takes pleasure in teaching you, and the harmonious strophes have troubled the attentive goatherds leaning over the crystal of fountains. Marsyas, Cybele is listening to you. The soul of your kisses is quivering in the waters.

"But the lover fled, the one who deceived you, the forgetful and wicked lover who mourned the death of Atys. But the lover fled and you followed her, and the flute has resonated for your dolors and your regrets. I hear the waters that are weeping, weeping your plaints.[1]

---

1 Lazare has run together the two well-known stories about Marsyas, involving the discovery of the *aulos* [a double pipe] discarded by Athene and his contest with Apollo, but his addition of an erotic element to Marsyas' brief following of Cybele and its possible relevance to the contest is unusual, and does not appear to come from classical sources. Such an involvement is, however, elaborately featured in the first part of an anonymous six-volume erotic work first published in 1726 called *Histoires secrete des femmes galantes de l'antiquité* [Secret His-

"Divine singer, ancestor of those who suffer, you deployed for dazzled humans the iridescent mantle of the world, and the world lived; your gesture created it. You revealed to us the obscure tendernesses, your voice instructed us of our confused terrors, it informed us of the candid pardon, dolorous Satyr, ancestor of those who suffer, and ancestor also of those who forgive.

"Those who were your disciples, and Olympus, which was dear to you, say that you paled when the orgiastic city Nysa loomed up before you, which surrounds the river of sobs. Undoubtedly, you understood that the marmoreal city was the place of refuge that the Moirai have developed for you, and you sat down near the partly-closed gate and moaned until morning. The echoes of Nysa repeated your distress.

"The constellations paled; the horses of the dawn reared up on the horizon; in the heavens their hooves raced and their manes rose in agitation, illuminating space. You closed your eyes, Marsyas; beyond doors standing ajar you had seen the God, and you crossed the threshold, for you did not want to elude fate. The river has conserved the pallor of your face.

"You had seen the God. You passed close to him without lowering your eyelids; you followed, slowly, the marble-flagstoned paths; then, on the Pnyx, you stopped. You leaned on the pedestal of a statue; it was Uranian Aphrodite whose benevolent gaze welcomed your coming. You took your flute and you sang. Oh, the waters have retained your religious prelude.

"The memory of the dear Phrygienne haunted your mind for an instant, the Phrygienne who fled from you,

---

tories of the Loose Women of Antiquity], with which Lazare might have been familiar.

and whom Apollo had conquered. No regret and no hatred survived in your heart. You related to yourself the delight of glad dawns, but you knew that they had vanished, and vanished too the evening of benevolent quietude, when you followed the queen of tenderness through the florid byways and the paths embalmed with vibrant odors. The murmur of the waters evokes their memory.

"Holocaust chosen by the tutelary Olympians, consecrated victim, Apollo advanced toward you. He mingled with the crowd that surrounded you; you perceived him, and Thanatos with the calm visage followed him, lifting his hand toward you. Then you proclaimed your renunciation and your sacrifice: the adored Phrygienne ceded to the rival god, and the flute henceforth your only lover, the mysterious flute, the voice of which spoke innumerable and profound and infinite words, the faithful and tender flute, the flute that the river still hears.

"Fearless rhapsodist, you have provoked the royal Archer. Apollo has smiled, and at his gesture the Pierides have descended, vigilant sisters, integral judges of combat. What prestigious melodies are yours, Marsyas, supreme host that poets mourn! The god himself listens to you, charmed. Sadly, he extends to you the sovereign Lyre, for the Destinies have spoken. Rebellious, you take the plectrum, and rebellious, you stroke the strings; they groan under your fingers, and the ineffable Musagete, after you, seizes the glorious shell, which spreads its triumphant harmonies. Dolorous Satyr, the memorable waters quiver, they quiver with your despair.

"Marsyas is vanquished, the Muses lament. Marsyas offers his hands to the inevitable bonds; the Scythian slave approaches, the tree of torture advances its boughs.

Marsyas is vanquished, the Muses lament! The slave has undressed the flute-player, his limbs are bound to the fatal trunk; the sharp reeds bite the flesh, they cleave the breast and the throat, and the blood springs forth, the expiatory blood of the one who wanted to equal the omnipotent god. The aegipans and the nymphs, the pastors of the plains and the goatherds of the hills have wanted to help Marsyas. They sob at the evil spectacle, the goatherds and the nymphs, the pastors and the aegipans. The waters weep their tears, the waters weep your blood.

"Marsyas is dead in the dusk. Marsyas is dead, who was vanquished. Marsyas has lived again in our memories: Marsyas, ancestor of those who suffer and those who forgive; happy goat-foot who renounced amour. His flute has been thrown into the frivolous waves of the Meander, and the skin of the singer, which the piety of humans retained, agitates when the pipes wake, but it remains bleak and silent when the victorious and cruel Lyre resonates. Marsyas is dead in the dusk; listen to the tears, listen to the blood.

"And you, Olympus, may your name be dear, for you have buried the Satyr, near Nysa, the city of the Orgiaste, on the bank of the river of dolors."

Euphorion stopped. He sat down on the periclinium strewn with petals, and, looking at Castus Pius, he said:

"Thus died Marsyas, for having touched the Lyre."

The Glory of Judas

To F. Bernard.[1]

What have I done, then, to be your chosen?
A. de Vigny.[2]

I

IN those times, Quintilla, zealatrice of Cain and prophetess of Judas, preached in Carthage, and in spite of
Tertullian, the impetuous presbyter, the Christians ran to
her and, in order to listen to her, quit the churches where
the true word was taught.[3]

She had chosen, in order to proclaim the culpable
doctrine, a grotto situated not far from the city, a grotto

---

1 Fernand, another of Lazare's younger brothers, born in 1866.

2 The Romantic poet Alfred de Vigny (1793–1863).

3 Tertullian's book *On Baptism* is couched as a reply to an unnamed
female Gnostic preacher of the "Cainite" cult. A sixteenth-century
translation named the preacher in question Quintilla, having appar-
ently borrowed the name mistakenly from a reference by St. Augustine
to an entirely different female preacher, but the name stuck and was
often repeated in subsequent references. Some Gnostic texts praised
Judas for his role in bringing about the redemption and considered
him the best of the disciples, but there is no way of knowing whether
Tertullian's Cainite held that view.

already soiled by the mysterious worship of abolished funereal gods. Still, on the walls, unknown characters could be distinguished, doubtless symbols of some infernal revelation or evidence of fallen fervors; and in the depths, a large marble table attested to redoubtable and criminal rites, for the marble was red and the blood of ancient sacrifices had stained it thus.

Now, that evening was a venerated anniversary. All that night was to commemorate the death to which the apostle whom the apostles had expelled from their company had consented, the voluntary death of Judas, the man of Karioth; and into the consecrated cavern flowed the faithful: men with long veils and men dissimulated behind the large flaps of their robes.

On the marmoreal altar Quintilla was seated, dressed in white; old men surrounded her. When the silent crowd had sat down, they intoned the ritual praises and customary hymns.

"Praised be Paul, who enlightened wisdom."

The auditors relied: "Paul, apostle and saint, be praised!"

The old men continued:

"Let us adore Paul, who was able to kill Saul, as Jesus felled Jehovah. Let us adore Paul, whom Sophia stole from Heaven. Let us adore Paul, who guided us toward the only God. Let us adore Paul, who guided us to Judas!"

"Let us adore Paul," murmured the audience; and the long sound of their invocations reverberated in muffled echoes in the lair.

A silence fell, and then the chorus of ancestral voices resumed, but lower, for the mystery of the spoken words filled the souls of those elders with fear.

"There is Sophia and there is Hystera!"[1]

With tremulous stammers of terror, the men alone repeated: "There is Sophia and there is Hystera!"

Then the oldest of the chorus-leaders, extending his hands—long, pale and stiff hands that seemed to be laying down a mantle of silence—pronounced the song imitative of the ineffable verities.

"Those who are called saints and who rename the evil book, the Bible, those who were rather the weak and the irresolute, Hystera formed: Abel, Jacob, Moses, a race of slaves incessantly curbed at the feet of the God who engendered evil and punished the powerful; Abel, the father of genuflections and vain sighs; Jacob and then Moses, vile conductors of a vile flock. Cursed be they, for before the cruel tamer of the world, they were cowards!"

"Cursed be they!" cried the old men.

"Those who are called wicked, and were contemptuous of the detestable book, the Bible, those who were rather the rebellious and the just, Sophia, eternal and infallible, created: Cain, Nimrod, Dathan, Korah, race of heroes incessantly struggling against him, Elohim, favorable to his humble worshippers. All of you also who sang in Sodom and rejoiced in Gomorrah, you who insulted Jehovah in Zeboim and the blasphemies in Abama,[2] warriors and sons of angels, you whom Sophia, sovereign and mother, inspired, glory to you, for before the cruel tamer of the world you were strong!"

---

1 Hystéra, which I have transcribed without the acute accent, was a neologism when Lazare devised it as a counterpart to Sophia [wisdom]. He presumably had the pseudo-medical term hysteria in mind rather than deriving the term directly from the Greek term for womb.

2 Abama features in some translations of *Ezekiel* 20:29; the A.V. has "Bamah," but the word in the original text is generally thought to be a common noun meaning "high place."

"Glory to you!" proclaimed the people, kneeling. "Glory to you!"

The acclamations, repeated by the rocks, rolled in waves of piercing sound, and then, like the distant rumbling of a storm, died down and faded away, and when the prostrated faithful rose to their feet, Quintilla was standing on the altar.

"Now," she said, "let the name be piously invoked of the supreme saint, the just man who underwent and accepted shame in order to deliver us from Hystera and Jehovah, the martyr who chose infamous and hideous death: the venerated name of the divine Judas."

"Blessed be Judas!"

Quintilla took a parchment from the marble and, holding up the scroll as the sacred law is held up in the synagogue:

"Here is the Gospel! The one that was revealed to Paul, the apostle with the benevolent heart, and which he wanted to write himself, in order to extract us from error. May his name be blessed because of that."

Like the waves of a calm lake stirred by an unexpected tempest, the crowd of auditors ran toward the prophetess, and all of them extended hands to touch the book, mere contact with which purified and instructed. But the old men stopped them and one of them cried:

"Listen!"

Having deployed the goatskin, Quintilla read, intoning the words in a rhythmic and bizarre chant, evocative of intense visions.

II

"Now, the son of Sophia, the vanquisher and master of Jehovah, Jesus, had suffered in his flesh. Arms extended, blessing the liberated world, he was dead; he had been resuscitated on the third day and, with his mother, he was henceforth enthroned.

"The disciples survived, spreading the doctrine, like a warm and sweet wine out of full amphoras: the great Paul and the venerable Peter; Luke and Mark, Matthew and John, the Lord's aedes, and Mathias, who replaced Judas the Holy, for destinies had to be accomplished.

"Since the consecrated deniers, the deniers struck by Ninus, the king of the Assyrians, had fallen into his hand, sealing the work, the elect of Karioth, ineffable criminal, wandered in the streets of Jerusalem, prey to insults and blows. The faithful of Christ gathered, in order to throw in his face the stones that the judges of the adulterous woman had dropped, and even Pilate and Caiaphas turned away from him scornfully. Everyone, the Galilean fishermen, brothers of those who had abandoned their nets on the shores of placid seas to follow the dear master, and the merchants who, henceforth, sold in peace under the porticos of the temple, refused his obol, fearing to touch the price of the adorable blood. Only one fearless Pharisee, one day, welcomed the Blessed One, and in exchange for the fatal sum, he sold him his field, the potter's field.

"Then, not having understood what inflexible laws had guided his soul, horrified by himself, Judas, the venerable traitor, took refuge in the enclosure of vines shaded by dense fig-trees. And that place, now sacred, Hakel-Dama, the bloody earth that pious lips will go to kiss, was situated to the south of the city, beyond the valley of Hinnom, and the Mount of Evil Counsel overlooked it.

"There, Judas lived alone, repenting of what he believed to be evil and bemoaning his imaginary sin. He nourished himself on roots and figs, drank the tepid and stagnant water of pools, slept on the pebbly ground bathed by his tears and silently implored the God that he had sent to Golgotha.

"One evening, sitting under the tall trees, he was praying desperately. The wind, perfumed by the aromas of the hills, awoke in his bruised heart the echo of divine parables once heard, when he accompanied the Anointed through the plains of Judea. And the heavy silence, which had sealed his lips for a long time, finally broke, and in a miserable voice he cried in the surprised night: 'I have sinned in delivering the innocent blood!' Spasmodic sobs raised his breast; he struck his head against the rugged trunks.

"Suddenly, an intense light invaded him; his eyes, the overly thick lids of which had closed, putting over each pupil a leaden cope, opened again, and he saw before him a man that he recognized. He had seen that white robe and that limpid visage so frequently, and that mouth had opened to pronounce friendly words so many times. He extended his trembling arms, and, shivering with anguish, he asked: 'Is that you, Rabbi?'

"Jesus replied: 'It's me.'

"The one who was desperate threw himself to the ground, and Christ, may his name forever be blessed in future centuries, lifted him up tenderly. He kissed him on the forehead and said to him: 'Judas, don't weep any longer.'

"Judas replied to him: 'I have lifted my hand against you, Master, and I have failed. Forgive me!'

"Again, the son of Sophia embraced him. 'The kiss that you gave me under the olive trees,' he said, 'I return to you, and as it freed me from terrestrial chains, let it free you from remorse.'

"Like a limpid flood, peace entered into the soul of the saint of Karioth, and Jesus, taking the hand that had received the liberating offering, continued: 'You have not sinned, Judas, you have accomplished a task.'

"'I have groaned, Rabbi, I have wept.'

"'Now, rejoice.'

"'My brothers, those who cherish you, have cursed me and chased me away.'

"'You shall be blessed in Heaven and you shall sit at my right hand.'

"'When you gave me bread, Satan seized me.'

"'It was necessary, you were designated. Already, my prophet Jeremiah had announced it.'

"'Why me, Lord?'

"'Be proud, Judas; at all times, I had chosen you. Those of my church believe that John was the dear apostle; no, the dear apostle was you; and if I have charged your name with opprobrium among men, it will be sanctified among the blissful. Only a few of those who live under my law will know your glorious destiny. It is necessary, for my triumph, that your ignominy persists.'

"'Master, dispose of your disciple whom your will rendered infidel.'

"'No one, after my mother, will be more welcome than you, Judas, for no one, in his terrestrial life, will have accumulated more insults.'

"'Now, they will be sweet to me.'

"'Son of Reuben, son of Cyborea,[1] I have wanted to curb you under the weight of sins, in order that, on the day of supreme revelations, the pride of the doctors will be confounded, and they will recognize that a criminal, like a sinner, works harder for salvation than them. When you floated over the waves, wailing, my protective right hand guided you to port; when you fled from the Queen, I guided you to Pilate; under the fatal apple tree, I directed your hand, which killed Reuben, your father, and I brought your mother Cyborea to you, whom you made your wife. The evening when, a parricide and incestuous, you came, weary of sin, to embrace my knees, I only received you in order that you might liberate me. Did I not say to you: *That which you must do, do it promptly?* At the appointed hour, you came, you by whom the eternal prophecies were to be confirmed, and your footsteps, in shaking the slopes of the garden of dolor, presaged the imminent redemption. Your lips, brushing my cheeks, were good to me, and good your betraying gaze, and I vowed the tenderest love to you for that. Listen now, preferred one.'

"'Speak, Lord.'

"'I wanted to descend again into Judea in order to calm your troubles and appease your dolor. Your tears lacerated me, and I have come to dry them up. But no one must know from your mouth what has been said. Finish what you have begun, and let your end justify your life.'

---

1 The idea that Judas' stepfather and stepmother were named Reuben and Cyborea, and the story of his fatal relationship with them, was popularized by a story included in Jacobus de Voragine's Medieval best-seller *Legenda Aurea* [The Golden Legend], a thirteenth-century compendium of the lives of the saints; it is an obvious adaptation of the ancient Greek legend featured in Sophocles' *Oedipus Rex*.

"With a benevolent gesture, Jesus placed his hand on Judas' head, which bowed and prayed. When he raised his head, he was alone in Hakel-Dama.

"The proffered words, eternal and immutable, were still floating in the air. They resounded in the soul of Judas, pure and beautiful, tearing away the veils that had previously darkened his mind. It was like a mist that, dissolving, had revealed the immensity of a marvelous pool, with a clear bed, a tranquil bank, and unperceived confines: a pool gemmed with large and solemn flowers. The Most Holy was reset in the infinity of the ages, he perceived his blessed predestination, he glimpsed the future austerities that had fallen to him.

"'Let your end justify your life,' the son of Sophia had said. His life had been filthy; he could not have the calm death of the Nabis. Abject in saintly fashion, he had lived by crime; by crime he had to perish. 'Do no murder,' was the precept that still resonated in Galilee, and was not the most frightful homicide the voluntary immolation of oneself?

"He understood the fatal order. He was the holocaust promised to the just holocaust. He had to accomplish the ultimate, criminal and meritorious oblation. The memory of past defilements reverberated in his utmost depths, like an antiquated chorus of evil voices, summoning the final defilement. He had raised his hand to Reuben, his father, and to Cyborea, his mother, and to Jesus, his God; he would raise it to himself.

"He marched toward the leprous cabin in which his broken pitcher lay and his clay bowls. He took a hempen rope, returned to the tall fig tree, and hanged himself from its groaning branches, pronouncing the name of the beloved betrayed.

"Profound harmonies floated over the trees and divine presences were revealed in the bloody field. Hyaline clarities dressed the bushes, supernatural corollas rained down on the hut, subtle perfumes trailed. And, abruptly, the body of the hanged man split down the middle and his entrails streamed on to the ground—it was necessary that his death be abominable—but his face was not tarnished by any stain, for he had touched the visage of Christ.

"The Eons assembled and the august Seraphim took Judas, who the opened heavens were summoning, and laborers who passed close to Hakel-Dama in the morning recounted the miserable expiation of the traitor, the man from Karioth.

"Judas, dear and designated victim, be blessed, thou art the liberator!

"Such were the things that the high wisdom revealed to Paul, apostle, when he was taken to the resplendent empyrean, and Paul, mysteriously, told to a few men, who conserved them, and promulgated them to the rare elect."

And, the secret, absolute and essential truths having been announced, Quintilla covered her face with the symbolic linen, and fell silent.

The Redemption of Ahasuerus

To Henri de Régnier.

Doubtless, his closed eyes beheld the plains of Paradise.
Pierre Quillard.

I

UNDER the weight of the anathema, the Jew wandered perpetually, and many dawns had risen since the morning when, on the hill, he had struck the man carrying the Cross; many dusks had sent the earth to sleep since old Adam had lifted the stone of his sepulcher to see a God die.

"Walk!" the Voice had said, whose ineffable accents the memory of the fugitive alone, in all the world, still reverberated. Ahasuerus had walked, and, when all those were dead who had known the Son of Man, he had remained curbed beneath the vision that his soul, alone, could henceforth evoke in its absolute verity. Heaped with opprobrium, covered in mud and spittle, he survived the collapse of empires, the abolition of beliefs and the annihilation of divinities; and, of all the centuries elapsed, he only retained one memory.

One day, a hermit had come to meet him, had prostrated himself before him and had kissed his cloak, because, for the ascetic, that assured man was the unique tabernacle in which the very word and the integral image of Jesus were preserved.

Since that moment, the Jew had felt his hatred slowly appeased, and his anger calmed. If he had not understood the immensity of the blasphemy, he had glimpsed the justice of the punishment, and his mouth having forgotten the insults, he went more calmly along the roads.

II

Now, this is the legend told by old monks retired to the depths of an oriental monastery, when, sitting under the palm trees in the evening, they mingle with the pilgrims.

One morning, in Judea, the dawn surprised the eternal voyager as he was climbing the slopes of the Mount of Olives. He traversed Bethany, descended the mountain, went into the valley of Jehosophat where Baal had once been worshiped, passed over the Cedron and arrived in Jerusalem. His heart filled with an incomprehensible anguish, he saw once again all the places that kept alive the memory of his crime: Golgotha, where a church now stood, the place of the Sepulcher, and sacred Calvary. He passed along the dolorous way, seeing again the passion forever glorified: here, Mary had encountered her son; there, the man from Cyrene had taken the Cross; further on, the holy women had wept and Berenice had wiped Jesus' face.

When night fell, Ahasuerus emerged from the city.

The obscurity was profound; the confused masses of the olive trees could hardly be distinguished, and when the wind inclined the foliage, one might have thought them great birds folding their wings. The Jew walked.

As on the evening of his flight, he heard the gorse along the path quivering mysteriously; voices sounded in his ears; breezes were born and extinguished; the dry grass rippled as if under the passage of reptiles; the ground rang, dully shaken by the accelerations that sometimes troubled a grave pace; and, brushed by invisible beings, caressed by plumages of an infinite softness, whipped by fabrics that flapped in the air, Ahasuerus tried in vain to penetrate the darkness. Like a blind man, he groped his way forward, extending his arm in front of him because he feared bumping into unknown forms.

Suddenly, in the distance, a crimson gleam appeared, showing the man the deserted road. Liberated from his dreads, he walked toward the light, and when he arrived near to Siloam, he realized that the glow was coming from the miraculous piscinas.

Alongside the reservoirs, not far from the place where the prophet was sawn in two, under a white mulberry bush, a beggar was sitting. He was clad in sordid rags, with large holes in places, allowing the sight of the leprosy with which his limbs, as well as his face, were covered. He was immobile; one might have thought him a statue if, in the visage that the malady had petrified, his eyes had not sparkled in a strange fashion. They were eyes of an ardent but indefinable color; at times they resembled flowing lava; the eyelids never blinked, and, ulcers having devoured the lashes and reddened the most delicate flesh, they were surprising, like two unusual jewels mounted in cornelian. The pupils were staring; they did not attract, they aspired, and when Ahasuerus received the impact of their gaze, he stopped in front of the leper. He contemplated him for a moment, and in his soul he felt, in spite of himself, an obscure and fatal pity awakening, when the mendicant spoke in a halting voice, the habitual stimulant of compassion.

"Whoever you are, aged wanderer whom hazard had brought toward a wretch forsaken by everyone, do not quit him without having relieved and rejoiced him with pious alms."

Driven by an invincible force, the fugitive, who had never actively sympathized, emptied his bag, in which a little dry bread and a few rare deniers were jostling, on to the supplicant's knees.

"Here," he said, "take without anger the insufficient offering of one who has nothing."

"Did not Jesus accept the widow's gift with more gratitude?" replied the leper.

Ahasuerus made a gesture of driving away obsessive thoughts.

"Have I offended you?" asked the beggar. "Is the name of God a bad augury for you? Are you not a Christian?"

The Jew did not reply. In response to the question posed, however, words of eternal repentance awoke in him; and his filthy interlocutor continued: "You're doubtless a Muslim pilgrim come to salute in Judea the tomb of Abraham the patriarch?"

"No," said Ahasuerus.

"Your feet are, however, soiled with ancient dust."

"Ancient," repeated the voyager; and, like a lamentable echo, he said again: "Ancient!"

"Your legs are buckling with lassitude; your back seems curbed by fatigue as much as by age. You must have been walking for a very long time."

"For a very long time," reiterated the Hebrew, and, in a hoarse sob, he murmured once again: "For a very long time."

"Are you not weary?"

"Weary?" murmured the accursed. "I'm very weary."

"Why always wander?"

"Why? Don't you know?"

Ahasuerus had not spoken his name, but he sensed obscurely that it was known to the mendicant and that, on the road, near the luminous piscina, his alms alone had been solicited.

"I know," said the leper. "I also know how unjust the punishment for the unwitting offense was."

"That's true. I didn't know God when I struck him."

"You believed him to be one of your fellows, the man who was climbing the hill, heavily laden?"

"Yes, certainly, one of my fellows."

"Was he not also a blasphemer?"

The Jew remained silent; he did not repeat the insult, and the strange mendicant continued: "You must have had enough of the monotony and the perpetual spectacle of days that are born and die?"

"The suns are too numerous, which for me have surged forth clad in roses, and sunk covered in gold; henceforth, their sight can no longer give me pleasure."

"Have you not desired death?"

"Death?"

"Yes, death—the death that would close your eyelids forever, which would lay you down forever beneath the beneficent clay, which would give you repose."

"Often, on the edges of towns, when I have seen the dead piously conducted, I have envied them. Many times, in traversing cemeteries, I have tried to slow my pace in order to savor for longer the amicable mildness of closed sepulchers; and the yews that incline gently over the cippi, the willows that make abandoned gestures over the tombs, the calm bushes of the pathways and the benevolent mosses that efface the lies of epitaphs, have murmured in my ear the initiatory words of an unknown peace."

"You would like to die, then?"

"Yes, but no one can strike me."

"I can."

"You?"

"Me. Do you doubt it?"

"Yes."

"However, since you encountered me on your route, you have remained motionless."

Dazed, Ahasuerus stared at the man who had arrested his paces. The man had grown, the crusts of his leprosy had fallen; his eyes were no longer red and lashless, but their brown irises shone with an unsustainable glare, and, like two magnets, they retained the Jew.

He wanted to flee, but he could not walk, and, terrified and trembling, he waited.

"Have no fear," said the fascinator. "I have taken pity on your suffering and I have come to liberate you."

"You're not Him, though?"

"Who do you mean by Him?"

"The only one who, it's said, can forgive; the one whom I struck, the one who punished me: Christ!"

At that proffered name the piscina extinguished its glittering waters. In the shadow, Ahasuerus could no longer distinguish anything but the eyes of the mendicant, whose stature had increased immeasurably. He heard his stammering voice.

"Tell me that you have lived too long."

"Yes, I have lived too long, since I committed the crime."

"Tell me that you would like to receive death."

"Yes, I would like to receive it—by my repentance."

"Listen."

"I hear you."

"Now that you have recognized God, blaspheme him, strike him again—there, beside you."

The Jew saw a cross loom up before him, dazzling in its brightness, and the Savior of the world agonizing upon it. Blood appeared to be flowing from his wounds, sweat steaming over the pale forehead, spreading over his meager breast, over his torn side and falling on to the cruelly pierced feet.

The fugitive recoiled.

"Strike," insinuated the Tempter.

Ahasuerus could no longer see him; he only heard his hissing words.

"Strike, and you shall have liberating death. You will no longer be a vagabond wandering the roads, dogs will no longer be able to bite your flesh with impunity, peasants will no longer expel you from their dwellings, children will no longer pursue you armed with sticks and stones. You will know sleep, the dreamless sleep."

"You're lying . . . perhaps."

"No, he has promised me himself that you will die."

The Jew took a step toward the crucifix. Jesus seemed to be extending his face toward him.

"Strike!" said the invisible counselor. "You will avenge yourself and liberate yourself."

But the hand of the Accursed was not raised.

"No!" he cried. "I don't want to die. I won't blaspheme, for Christ is God!"

A snigger resounded in the air, accompanied by the sound of flight. Ahasuerus heard crowds around him once again; once again he was brushed by wings, and scales rattled beneath his feet. Then everything fell silent; a pure light emerged from the piscinas, and the arms of the cross, broadening, touched the sky.

"When you wish it," said Ahasuerus, "I shall perish, but as yet I have not expiated my sin. I have failed. I ought to suffer. All the spittle I have received in my incessant course cannot efface that with which the legionaries covered you, and the rods that fall on my back are not heavy enough for the sin committed. I shall continue to walk the roads, as a penitent and not as a vagabond. At every hour, I shall bless you because you are punishing me, and blessed will be the day when you call me to you, forgiven."

Having spoken, the Jew cut a branch from the tree that had sheltered Isaiah and, with a firm stride, he returned toward the city.

III

That night, a Coptic priest coming from Bethany saw auroral gleams resplendent in the air; he heard prodigious voices that were singing hymns, the meaning of which he divined without hearing the words, and he understood clearly that they were the sacred cohorts.

He stopped, knelt down, and kissed the ground devotedly; when he raised his head, he saw white legions of angels bearing psalteries. They were surrounding a resplendent chariot, which was rising up slowly. In the chariot, an old man was seated, wearing a crimson robe, haloed by a flamboyant nimbus; and the Coptic priest, who had once given alms to that old man, recognized him.

It was Ahasuerus, redeemed, who was rising up to Heaven.

The Descendants of Iskander

To A. Bernard.[1]

What has become of those individuals
who were making so much noise?
　　　　The life of Chateaubriand.

I

THE jujube-trees had reflowered many times since Rajah Souran, grandson of Iskander-Dhou'l-Karnein,
the master of the double horn,[2] had descended into the

---

1 Armand, the youngest of Lazare's three younger brothers, born in
1870.

2 Iskander, Iskandar or Eskandar is the name given to Alexander the
Great in various Persian writings. He was often identified by Medieval
scholars with the character Dhul-Qarnayn [literally, "the two-horned
one"] featured in the Quran as the builder of a wall to contain Gog
and Magog; the (entirely spurious) identification led to the conqueror
sometimes being cited in literature as "the two-horned Alexander."
The Malay epic *Hikayat Iskandar Zulkarnain*, which probably dates
from the seventeenth century, recruits the hero as an ancestor of a
royal dynasty of Sumatra via various kings previously mentioned in
the sixteenth-century *Malay Annals*, including Raja Suran and Demang
Lebar Daun, King of Palembang, whose daughter was Wan Sendari;
the land of Kling and other incidental details of the story also appear
to be derived from the *Malay Annals*.

kingdoms of the sea; many autumns had stripped their branches since Rajah Souran had departed for the land of Kling; and now King Demang Liber Daoun reigned over the soil of Andala.

Near Perlambang, in the middle of the river Malayou, rose a hill. The waters surrounded it with a girdle of changing colors, for at night, under the moon, the water was white; when the dawn quivered, it was tinted pink; it turned a harsh cobalt blue at noon, and sunsets covered it with gold, while twilights tinted it with hyacinth and tender gray. The slopes of the hill were bristling with bamboos, in the midst of which rose reeds helmed with a pale down; between the bamboos, rice-fields were displayed. At the very top, on the plateau that overlooked the town, palm trees loomed up. Under the shelter of their leaves, a cabin covered with laths was huddled.

Two young women lived there. In the morning they cultivated their rice-field, and when evening came, sitting on a wooden bench in the shade of great trees, they watched the sun, which forsook the river to set ablaze the orchards overlooking the city, and, from there, to plunge into the distant sea, whose foam they could perceive confusedly.

They had never known their father or their mother; even the memory of the day that they had come to that locale had fled. Both of them were blonde, and their complexion was gilded like bronze brightened by dazzling fires. They always went barefoot; no fabric oppressed their breasts, which surged forth, rounded like amber cups. Their twin beauty would have disconcerted the search for dissimilarities if the eyes of the elder had not been green and the irises of the younger dark brown. One was named Rahu and the other Visena.

Rahu and Visena knew that valiant and handsome warriors lived in the city with the thousand terraces, but they had never descended to the banks of the river in order to see them, for they also knew that the future lovers for whom they were waiting were not among them.

Now, one night when the two sisters were both asleep, they were woken up by a strange noise; it was like the clear sound of shields resonating under the impact of blades. They looked through the door, always open, and perceived a bright light on the hill. The bamboos were burning like torches; the reeds were topped by luminous plumes, and the flames descended all the way to the river, whose waves were flowing golden.

"Do you see?" asked Rahu, in a low voice. "Might it be Indra, descended to the earth?"

"If Indra were advancing," Visena replied, "we would not be so tremulous, and we would be delighted by his approach. Perhaps it's the Great Serpent, which has come to deposit its gems nearby."

Amid the foliage, the miraculous fires were still burning. One by one, the trees along the river bank were ignited; the palaces of Perlambang were illuminated by red glows; on the horizon, the ocean was on fire.

"I'm afraid," Rahu murmured.

"I'm afraid," stammered Visena.

They hid their heads under the mantles of their loose hair; dying of fright, they hugged one another and, after long hours of anguish, they went to sleep

In the morning, when the sun emerged from the mists, they woke up and, without wishing her sister the habitual good morning, Rahu said: "Let's go see the fire that was burning on the hill last night."

"Let's go," replied Visena.

They got dressed, washed their eyes with the dew of flowers, placed a white cluster of jasmine in their hair and set forth. They traversed the little wood in which birds were singing in the foliage. The Apsaras had shed the beads of the necklaces over the blades of grass, and there were some as pink as coral, as blue as lotus, as green as the tresses of lianas, and some brighter and more limpid than those coming from the land of Kling. There were some that were gilded like Rahu's face, others had the pale color of Visena's feet, and there were some in which the liana-green, the lotus-blue and the coral-pink were combined. Rahu and Visena took a few of them delicately in their fingertips; they placed them on the gauze of their corsages, and a few slid though to pose on their breasts.

The two sisters continued their route, for their field was a long way from the cabin, on the bank of the river, behind the mango-trees. No light was evident any longer. They went on, and, from time to time, they perceived blonde waters constellated with nenuphars.

Suddenly, Rahu cried: "Look!"

The light had reappeared, and they stopped, gripped by amazement. In their field, the rice had suddenly grown. The leaves were silver, the stems chrysocale;[1] the grains, as big as jujubes, were rubies, and in all directions, the marvelous rice-field was spreading light, crimson, white and russet.

That's what we saw last night, thought the young women.

---

1 I have left the word "chrysocale" as it appears in the original rather than translating it into chrysocolla, the usual English word for the mineral known by that name in French, because it is used again later in the story as if it were the name of a plant.

They advanced further on the hill, where the earth had taken on the color of gold, and on the metallic soil, in the shade of three fig-trees isolated on the slope, they perceived three young men. They were very tall, their faces had the warm tint of bronze, their noses curved proudly, and on the blood of their mouths brown moustaches curled. They wore regal garments; their foreheads were circled by diadems. One of them was mounted on a white ox, he surpassed the other two by a cubit; the second was standing to his right, holding a sword whose pure steel was shining; the third, armed with a long pike, stood to his left.

"Who are you?" asked Rahu.

"Where have you come from?" Visena asked.

One of the young men, the one who was astride the ivory-hued ox, replied: "We are the sons of King Rajah Souran and Princess Mah-Tab-al-Bahri, and we descend from the glorious Iskander, Emperor of countries of the Occident and the Orient. My name is Sang; the one brandishing the sword is named Kisna, and Ivakou in the one bearing the spear."

"It is a long time," said Rahu and Visena, "since the Emperor Iskander and Rajah Souran returned toward Indra. How have you, whose ancestors they were, arrived in the land of Andala?"

Sang made a gesture and Kisna spoke.

"When our father quit the kingdom of the sea; when, mounted on a marine horse, he came to reign again over the world, he said to King Aktab, from whom we descend: 'King, when my sons have grown, you will take them to the terrestrial shores. Thus will be perpetuated, until the end of time, the race of the great Iskander.' The years have gone by, the designated day has come, and we have emerged from the profound ocean; then, guided by protective gods, we have walked to this hill, and you have come toward us, whiter than the foam, rosier than the dawn, more gilded than the sunset."

Rahu and Visena smiled and, troubled by their beauty, Kisna let the blade waver, and Ivakou allowed the spear to lower.

But the two sisters questioned: "How can we believe you?"

At a sign from Sang, Ivakou replied:

"Can you not see, maidens with beautiful eyes, that we are crowned with diadems? Look around us; the silvery earth will tell you that it bears the sons of ancient kings, and the rutilant ears will tell you that they are saluting the children of Iskander."

Rahu and Visena bowed, and in their soft voices, they said: "Princes, we were expecting you. Come with us."

They set forth on the march. Rahu and Visena went on ahead, virginal announcers; on their breasts, the pearls of the Apsara shone more purely, and the bamboos let forgotten gems rain down upon them. Then came Sang, astride the ox; behind the prince marched Kisna and Ivakou; they clinked the sword against the spear, the spear against the sword, and the cortege went on to the martial sounds of that music. The waters of the river splashed in joyful cascades; the mango-trees on the bank stood taller; the jasmines spread sweeter perfumes; the birds sang more brightly; triumphant harmonies were propagated in the branches; even the sun scintillated with a marvelous glare, and under the footfalls of the heroes and the young women, the hill quivered.

They arrived at the solitary cabin; there, sitting on a carpet made of leaves, they ate the frugal foodstuffs offered by the bikang and the jujubes, and drank milk. Then Sang told strange stories of mysterious marine countries; Visena sang the glory of Nouchiveran the Just, King of the West and the East;[1] and when evening came, Rahu celebrated the omnipotence of Indra. Then, under the rustic roof of laths, they all went to sleep.

II

The next day, when the princes woke up, Rahu and Visena put on rose-colored robes and mantles with changing hues. Crimson grains of rice sparkled in their hair; silver leaves glittered in their ears, and having twisted chrysocale stems several times, they had disposed them around their arms and ankles. Thus adorned with divine jewels, they bowed to their guests and went down the hill, going to the city to announce the coming of the grandsons of Iskander.

They arrived in the vicinity of the river. As soon as they appeared, two black swans advanced, curbing their long dark necks. They seemed to be saying to the young women that they had been waiting for them for a long time. Rahu and Visena caressed their nocturnal plumage; they sat down in the cradle of their soft wings, and the magical birds conducted them to the banks; then they took flight and disappeared into the splendors of the empyrean.

Under the trees aligning their columns and arches along the banks, Rahu and Visena perceived an ivory chariot; it was harnessed to two gazelles, which approached, bending

---

1 Nouchiveran was a legendary king of Persia.

their legs in a sign of submission. The two sisters took their places on the seat, and the carriage progressed along paths lined by flowering pomegranates.

Soon, in the distance, the city appeared. It was protected by a wall nine brasses high, built in polished black stone. The skill of the architects had been such that, the joints between the dark blocks being invisible, the ramparts resembled immense mirrors. The gates were pure steel, enriched with precious metals that formed rare and subtle arabesques, and rising suns set the walls and the closed gates ablaze, enlacing Perlambang in a wild ocean of gold.

Within the enclosure, the protective towers surged forth first, and then seven hills rose up, with flanks laden with palaces, temples and gardens. They were disposed in a circle, and in the middle slept a vast lake populated by fishes with monstrous heads. The lake was surrounded by a bushy park. There, mimosas with palpitating foliage shivered; soapberry trees swung their long yellow clusters; djambous sagged, violet with flowers and rosy with fruits. In the shade of palm trees the strange corollas of corylopsis were flamboyant; the troubling perfumes of caladiums soared. Amid the tangles of lianas, the backs of wild beasts often undulated; the tread of elephants oppressed the carpet of dry leaves, and the flight of antelopes agitated the bamboos.

Over the slack waves of the pool extended a steep island veiled with verdure. Access to it was granted by three stairways; one was in white agate; maidens and wives went by that route; the steps of the second were in crimson stone, only trodden by warriors and priests; the third caused its golden steps to shine, having only ever seen rajahs and sovereigns pass by. Simple wooden ladders disposed here and there sufficed for the common people and servants.

In the center of the island rose the King's palace, staging its marble terraces and stairways. At the corners of ramps, chimerical beasts with hideous faces grimaced; innumerable galleries deployed their jade columns, and an army of pillars with a thousand forms surprised the eyes. Silver balconies overhung the porticos; towers were topped with broad belvederes that overlooked the land of Andala, and gardens were spread out at the base. They were sparkling with sumptuous flowers, and the winds that agitated the censers and ewers caused the air to quiver with unfamiliar scents.

Lacquered pavilions were mirrored in basins decked with gems and murmuring with the impact of jets of perfumed water. On the lawns, rare birds were marching; they illuminated the emerald carpet with their vermilion copes, while domesticated tigers passed by, grave, pensive and melancholy.

Rahu and Visena went through the gates and penetrated into the city; a crowd assembled, surprised. Then they stopped the candid gazelles, and shouted, three times:

"People of Perlambang, the sons of Iskander have come!"

They came to the edge of the great lake and there they said:

"Sovereign of Andala, very noble rajah, the sons of Iskander have come!"

Seated in the great hall of the palace, on the imperial throne laminated with bronze and encrusted with pearls, King Daoun heard the words, and sent his guards to fetch the women who were preceding the heroes. A silver boat set forth from the island; it reached the shore and the young women descended into it. The vessel headed toward the agate stairway, but the oarsmen were unable to steer the boat as they wished; in spite of their efforts it came to rest at the foot of the royal stairway, and Rahu and Visena, in the splendor of the midday, climbed the golden steps.

They were taken to the rajah, and he said to them: "Who are you, strangers, who, in coming to see us, have arrived by the route of queens?"

They both bowed and, smiling, they replied:

"My name is Rahu."

"I am named Visena."

"From what country do you come?" asked the King. "What gods have chosen you to announce the birth of the glorious sons of Iskander?"

"For a long time," said Rahu, "we have been dormant on the hill over there, in the middle of the river, and we have never descended into the towns; we have never seen warriors."

"Before the handsome young men issued from Dhou'l-Karnein," sighed Visena.

Rahu then recounted the miracles of the night: the earth becoming the color of gold, the silver foliage, the precious ears of corn, and the arrival of the ephebes.

King Daoun summoned the fakirs and prophets. He interrogated them; the holy men replied that they had known this for a long time. They had known that a day would come when princes, heirs of the Master with the double horn, would emerge from the ocean to mingle their illustrious blood with the blood of the emperors of Andala, and they declared that it was necessary to go to the hill to seek the expected princes.

III

That evening, when the sun inclined toward the sea, the drum Sarama was beaten seven times, and the trumpet sounded seven times. The rajah descended from the palace with his daughter, and the lords and ladies of his court. The junks transported them to the other shore, and there a cortege formed.

Rahu and Visena were the foremost, in their ivory chariot drawn by the gazelles. Behind them advanced warriors bearing lances ornamented with the tails of cows. After that came the common people, clad in variegated fabrics and waving brightly-colored fans. Then danced the herald who was striking the sacred gong; he was accompanied by a flute-player; to his left the trumpets resonated, to his right the cymbals vibrated and the drums burst forth. Further away, the standards palpitated, followed by pages, who were carrying royal insignia on cushions. Then the triumphal palanquin appeared. It was made of precious odorous wood, curiously sculpted, decorated with gems; white plumes covered it, extracted from the wings of huge foreign birds and brought by black men. It was carried on the shoulders of the most illustrious men in the realm. Before the palanquin marched the great officers and the bodyguards, with naked swords; the pikes of soldiers glittered to either side.

Everything seemed finished, but soon dancers enveloped in gauze approached, and the voices of women were heard. They were singing in a strange fashion, celebrating the virtue of their queen, and when they had passed by, the daughter of the rajah, Princess Sendari, was seen advancing, mounted on an elephant covered with sumptuous drapes. A white robe and a mantle woven in gold cloth enveloped her; innumerable bracelets were resplendent on her arms and ankles: simple silver rings, dragons with bloody eyes, dazzling circlets of precious stones, serpents with emerald scales, yellow lizards beneath topaz flames. Her ears were ornamented with fabulous diamonds; in her brown hair a diadem was set, and pearls disposed in tightly placed rows covered her forehead, descended along her cheeks and came to fall upon her cleavage.

Sendari's fingernails were tinted with henna; her lapis eyes were enlarged by a circle of bistre; her lips were bloodied with carmine; her delicate nostrils were lightly blurred and her face was radiant with a divine majesty.

In Sendari's wake marched maidens and wives, and guards surrounded them.

They quit Perlambang and, when they had traversed the river, they climbed the flanks of the hill, while beneath the orange-tinted rays of the setting sun, banners and iridescent parasols caught fire.

When they reached the plateau, in front of the cottage, thy saw Sang astride his ox; Kisna and Ivakou were at his sides. Rahu and Visena, who had arrived first, were already kneeling. Sang raised his hand, his brothers struck the sword against the spear. The two young women cried: "Listen!"

The flutes and cymbals fell silent.

"King," said the Prince, "nobles, priests, warriors, merchants and people, the grandsons of Iskander have come to you."

The people and the merchants, the warriors and the priests, the nobles and the King proclaimed: "Salvation be upon you!"

The rajah emerged from his palanquin, Sang descended from his mount, and they advanced toward one another. To honor the sovereign of Andala, the Prince bowed, but Daoun conducted him toward the Princess, and Sendari curtsied. Then the trumpets burst forth, clamors rose up and cries of joy were heard resounding all the way to the horizons; the gongs resounded, the drums were beaten; the priests sang royal hymns and the dancers performed triumphant steps.

For forty days and forty nights, fêtes were celebrated on the hill, for King Daoun had accomplished the old prophecies. He had married Sendari, his daughter, to the magnificent Sang, and Rahu became the wife of Kisna, and Ivakou married Visena.

Thus, in accordance with the word of Rajah Souran, emperor of the marine kingdoms, the descendancy of the great Iskander was perpetuated.

The Ineffable Lie

To Marcel Collière.[1]

The best thing is to hear again
the only words that can delight us.
Villiers de l'Isle Adam.[2]

I

AT dawn, the prophet was taken to the public square, preceded by mummers who mimicked his convulsions of despair. He had been coifed with a heavy iron tripod the form of which simulated the tiara of pontiffs, and his white robe had been tainted with wine lees, thus appearing a derisory crimson. He was obliged to remain exposed to the insults and spittle of the populace, under the protective guard of cohorts, until dusk, for royal clemency had decided that the man, although a knave, should

---

1 Marcel Collière (1863–1932) only published one volume of verse, *La Mort de l'espoir* [*The Death of Hope*] (1888), but he was a member of the Mikhaël/Lazare clique, and an associate of Pierre Quillard, one of whose plays he helped to produce in 1891.
2 The Comte de Villiers de l'Isle Adam (1838–1889) was greatly admired by the young Symbolists as a pioneer of literary decadence and an important popularizer of the *conte cruel.*

admire the splendor of the day once more. However, the priests had excited that royal benevolence themselves; they knew how much more anguishing death is in the twilight, when no light comes to solicit hope and appease fear. When the sun disappeared, the annunciator of the new faith was to die.

One morning he had surged forth from unknown countries. At crossroads where people gathered, in the middle of stairways encumbered by the curious, in arenas filled with crowds, he had spoken, and everyone had listened to him, surprised and charmed. He had spoken about love and tenderness, about sublime abnegations and joyful sacrifices; he had promised the appeasement of terrors; he had depicted distant but sure happiness.

Women and children, old men and the humble, had acclaimed him; captivated by his words they had gone to him, saluting him with the name of Master. They were greatly afflicted by ennui. The ancient beliefs, in decline for a long time, could no longer satisfy them, and the resuscitated past had been no more sufficient for them; their souls, devoid of fallen religions, wanted to see the light again. They were disgusted with the familiar milieux, the customary agitations; their weary thoughts fell asleep in dreams of annihilation or dissipated in vain impatience.

The rich quit the city. They paraded their own ennui in the country; soon, sated, they went to bury themselves in the hearts of forests, and they deserted the forests in order to sleep close to shores caressed by the warm sea. Then, the soporific calm of the waves having become insupportable to them, they returned to the cities, where the cries of the circus and the sight of blood reanimated them. Others, in their desire for the unknown, sought unrealizable sensualities, but their senses were not sufficient for the enjoyments of which they dreamed.

Then, when nothing any longer tempted them, when even the suffering of others only procured them a temporary excitement, they thought about killing themselves in order to feel, at the supreme moment, their hearts beating faster, at the same time as the glimpsed afterlife embraced them with a delicious dread. Death was the conqueror of pleasure, which always escaped. However, if some only waited on their own death-throes as an unexperienced thrill, others, the poor, felt nothing but the fear of the unknown looming up before them, and fear paralyzing their ultimate gasps. To those, the prophet brought peace and joy.

Tranquillized by his words, those anxious for the future neither summoned death nor desired it more. When it came, they welcomed it as a liberating friend, bringing, according to them, ecstasies for which they had hoped; and they deserted the temples, no longer bringing impotent divinities the tribute of their long-indifferent genuflections.

But the priests of the dead gods, the sacrificers and the hierodules who lived in the depths of the sanctuaries, in the adoration of abolished glories, had risen up against the blasphemer. They had launched their anathemas against him, they had pursued him and had him condemned, doubtless believing that the blood spilled would attest to the reality of their dream—and now, in the square, in expectation of the torture, the man was standing.

Before him filed a ferocious throng. Old men insulted him as the killer of ancient faiths; philosophers addressed mocking speeches to him; merchants abused him—they hated him particularly, for he had proclaimed the vanity of luxury—and some, more reckless, struck him with their staffs. Slaves and castrati, finding him too handsome, threw stones at him; women, lustful or conscienceless, ashamed of his virtue or simply cruel, covered him with ordure, and mothers lifted up their little children, who tugged the prophet's beard, smiling. Debauchees, come running to see suffering, plunged long pins into his cheeks; actors, jealous of his renown, excited their dogs against him; and young men had come from distant regions in order to torture the man of whom they were weary of hearing talk.

However, a word of pity sometimes emerged from the crowd; timidly sympathetic hands were raised to wipe the martyr's face; matrons extended water to his thirsty mouth; maidens had used their veils to remove spittle and mud. In the evening, when the sun was weeping its last crimson tear in the Occident, a courtesan approached the Master and kissed his lips piously, without hearing the laughter of the people, who believed it to be a derision.

Suddenly, a gong sounded; that was the signal. The priests, clad in white, red or yellow robes, according to the cult, emerged from the temples in long processions and came to collect the disparager of their gods in order to take him outside the gates; the city ought not to be soiled by the blood of an impious individual. One final time the chief scribe read the sentence:

"In the name of the omnipotent Immortals, just punishers of blasphemies, the enemy of religions will be exposed for an entire day in the public square and consigned to the execration of the zealots of the true faith. At dusk, he will be taken to the accursed place into which parricides are cast, and there, he will die the death prescribed for sacrilege. No one may approach the victim during the hours of his agony."

The condemned man smiled and said: "I am ready." In a lower tone he murmured: "The time has come."

The cortege set forth.

<h2 style="text-align:center">II</h2>

In the middle of the valley so many times polluted by the last gasps of criminals, a high wall stood; it was made of large blocks of stone bristling with sharp hooks, and so much blood had flowed over them that one might have thought they were made of somber porphyry. There, the man had been taken, and he agonized all night, his sides pierced by two iron points and his armpits pierced by two others. At his feet, the soldiers of the cohorts were lined up, containing the crowd; their torches splashed their helmets and breastplates with red gleams; sometimes an abrupt flame rose up, illuminating the fact of the victim; clamors then emerged from the mob; when they had fallen silent, belated sobs were heard.

From time to time, men and women advanced, thrown forward by an eddy, but the guards repelled them, for fear that one of the faithful might reach the wall, and, by his mere presence, appease the anguish of the man who had been condemned to die without having a pious friend nearby.

Shortly before dawn, however, a disciple—the one that was the most cherished—succeeded in getting through the iron hedge and, without being seen, came to prostrate himself before the dying man. He stayed there for a long time, weeping and receiving the blood of the wounds in his hair. Then he raised his head and said: "Master."

The Master replied: "What do you want with me?"

The disciple continued: "Have pity on me and forgive me, for dread has not quit me. After having extracted me from the darkness, after having guided me on to the right path, you said to me: 'Go forth and continue my work.' I cannot. At this supreme moment, when you are attesting the truth by your suffering, when I am receiving the aspersion of your blood, redemptive as that of the ram or the bull never was; at this moment, I no longer believe."

The Annunciator lowered his head; a tear fell upon the hands extended toward him, and in a strange voice he replied: "What does it matter?"

"What did you say?" exclaimed the supplicant.

"Shut up," replied the Inspired. "Listen. Certainly, I believed that I would die without having revealed my secret; I hoped to carry away with me the thought that has burned my soul; destiny has decided otherwise; I shall speak. I have ordered you to depart after my death, to go barefoot and to proclaim the revealed God everywhere. I order you to do so again, and I say to you: what does your incredulity matter, since I myself have never believed?"

"You!"

"Me. You do not understand me, you are not a veritable apostle. What are you seeking? Peace of mind; the means of attaining death without trembling; and perhaps you would even like to replace the terror of the last minute with I know not what egotistical joy. Leave that to the humble and the weak, then; do as I do. For a long time I have meditated; the doubt has only gripped me more profoundly. One day, I recognized the vanity of my quest, and alone, desperate, I traveled the roads as a vagabond. Weary of savants and philosophers, I sought out the ignorant; I encountered the unfortunate. Around me I saw suffering, and a profound pity seized me before the human herd, wandering without guides or sustenance. They dragged out their lamentable lives, bearing their burdens and supporting their ulcers, without a single ray of joy coming, like a consoler, to touch their souls. I wanted to give them peace. I went to them, and I said to them: 'Love one another; that is the new faith; that is the veritable law; that is the true God.' And they believed me. Consoled henceforth, they knew peaceful evenings and mornings full of hope, and I kept for myself the grim nights, the sufferings and the lacerations of existence, the redoubtable fear of the end."

And in a lower voice, for he was dying, the martyr proffered these words: "Go, poor anxious heart, and if you cannot abolish dolor in yourself, proclaim to others that it will only be a vain dream for them, if they want to believe in our words. Adieu."

The disciple stifled his plaint. He stood up, and in the nascent dawn he cried: "The prophet is dead who appeased anguish. I have come to tell you, like him: 'Love one another; that is the new faith; that is the veritable law; that is the true God.'"

The body of the victim stood out with a pure whiteness against the somber wall. In the crowd, the faithful extended their arms toward him, and their clamors of distress glorified the man who had died for them, and for the truth.

The Advent

It is that shadow alone that you love.
                        Villiers de l'Isle Adam.

I

IN what country? Mysterious or precise, distant or near, veiled by mysterious mists, illuminated by warm light? Everywhere, perhaps, and also nowhere. In a country.

On a flamboyant day, a day of supreme annunciation, the air resounding with mystic harmonies, mingled with anguished cries, joyful sounds, indecisive rumors, satisfied sighs. On a day desired, but finally accomplished.

In a square surrounded by abject houses and princely palaces; a square whose vision would have been reminiscent of the memory of multiple cities, and yet of none.

And in that country, on that day, in that square, a confused crowd, gravely happy or serenely sad, impatiently placid, waiting for something known and yet unknown: a lie or a truth.

A platform was erected there, draped with red and black, a legible symbol; on the platform, a man, handsome, with a disquieting beauty, clad in a garment of faded color, as likely a pontifical dalmatic as a warrior's tunic. The man was about to speak, as the solicitous expectation of the crowd bade him do. He spoke.

"People," he said, "this hour is an hour of joy."

At those words, which liberated the listeners from their uncertainty, triumphant clamors resounded and reverberated in strident echoes, all the way to the mountains that surrounded the city with the blue wave of their ridges.

The man who had proffered the words made a gesture, the cries ceased, dying away into a musical murmur, and he continued.

"For centuries without number, you hoped for this happy moment, when the hero to whom all mysteries belong would come to tell you: 'The man for whom your anxious souls have been waiting has finally arrived.' Many a time, deceived by the force of your desires, scorning the will of the omniscient, you have run to impostors. Like lambs deceived by the bells of fallacious sheepfolds, you thought to find the shelter where your spirits could go to sleep, weary of having suffered, for you were suffering."

A dolorous plaint was heard, the echo of ancient and ever renewed suffering; a strident plaint, like the appeal of sad and implacable buccinas.

"Henceforth," the man continued, "you have finished with lying hopes; infallibly, the light will shine for you. The savior affirmed by your forefathers, the one whose advent has been sung by divinely inspired poets, the one whom veritable miracles ought to salute, the Savior is born. The propitious stars, whose progress has been surveyed by priests in the depths of sanctuaries, are announcing the happy day. The two precursors proclaiming the master have surged forth among us, and on a clear night, when new flowers embalmed the rejuvenated earth and unknown constellations shone in the sky, someone opened the doors of the temple with his redemptive hands, and we prostrated ourselves before him, for he really was the promised victor."

And in a forceful chorus, they all replied: "He is the promised victor."

And as they hoped for the relief of their pains, they exalted that unknown individual, whom they knew by virtue of having desired him for such a long time:

"Glory to you, liberator of our sick bodies." Some added: "Pacifier of our troubled minds."

"Be blessed, you who will conquer terrestrial felicities for us." Others continued: "You who will lift the stone of the sepulcher in which our souls are confined."

The laudatory chant filled the air. The wind sowed the rhythms on the mountains and the plains, which the lairs and the rocks repeated. But the herald of holy things, standing on the scaffold hung with red and black, listened with a mysterious smile to the habitual sobbing, the voice of age-old trees, which had not ceased in the forests. When everyone fell silent, his voice resonated again.

"Yes, rejoice! Declare the death of evil and the victory of sovereign delights, and that the resounding hymn of triumph is finally realized. Fortunate are you; you shall know the final word, without having known the terrors of research; and the honey of your science will not be worth as much as the pure balm of the chosen Word. The pontiffs have had their day; their domination is abolished, for the veil that hid the sanctuary is open now for all."

Like a host of hornets, malicious sounds of joy flew up from the crowd. The sages and the priests, possessors until that day of unfathomable secrets, were hated; they marched placidly in the midst of dolorous paths, and their serenity seemed to spoil the happiness for which men had waited in vain. So the pride of no longer owing anything to divine rhapsodies or to omnipotent mystagogues augmented the supreme and unexpected spectacle of their humiliation and their downfall. The entire people blessed the God, breaker of gods; vibrant voices cried to the revelator: "Speak!"

He continued speaking.

"You, the Rich, in luminous palaces around tables laden with meat and illustrious wines, who know anxieties, biting your hearts like black dogs; you whom malady grips daily at feasts, changing you laughter into a rictus; you who know the dread of fortunes too soon dissipated, and miseries harsher than the customary poverty of the humble, since they come like rapid clouds to darken the stars; you shall henceforth have perpetual serenity and the end of fears will inundate your souls with a durable and benevolent gaiety, like candid shores bathed by an ever-equal tide."

The acclamations of the rich saluted those promises. Forgetting their ulcers and their present woes in the vision of a future filled with joyful flowers, they exalted in that imminent happiness, and some, crippled, lying on litters borne by slaves, sat up, fleetingly cured. But the poor murmured dully. That assurance annihilated their most cherished dream, the one that they had been forming for countless days: the dream of seeing their oppressors oppressed in their turn—for there was not one of them, no matter how abject, who had not dreamed of having one of those magnificent individuals under his table, where he would be nourished on scraps. Suddenly, they fell silent; the envoy had turned toward them.

"Poor," he said, "poor, dear to God: beggars whom the summer sun overwhelms and the winter forests kill; slaves huddled in ergastules, servants curbed under inclement yokes, workers bent by incessant labor; you whom the torture of hunger, your frightful queen, and death, your pale cavalier, harass rudely, you shall no longer suffer. Henceforth you shall have, with the forgetfulness of hours in the banished evil, eternal happiness. The winds will appease their drilling bite. They will surround your bodies with subtle effluvia and soft caresses, and you will sleep, cradled by their perfumes, in the vernal durance of a beloved season."

The poor silenced their secret rancor then; their voices rose up, celebrating in puerile exclamations the imminent felicities. Young men looked more ardently at their lovers and spouses embraced; through kisses they had known the forgetfulness in which chagrins go to sleep, like white hands curing wounds; they went forth to find infallible amour. But the rich complained loudly; the woes of the humble had previously been half their satisfaction, and they wondered whether pleasures could be, without the sobs that were for them benevolent stimulants.

The annunciator, on the somber and bloody platform, continued, ironically:

"However, whoever you are, powerful or oppressed, do not think to find the supreme realities here, for the liberator of your bodies is charging your souls with heavy chains of duty thus far misunderstood. At his voice, the messenger of divine orders, you will understand that empty is the joy, and inane the dolor, that sublunar mirages trail after them. You will know that dolors and joys, or, rather, the sensations that appear to you to affirm themselves thus, only exist in the mirror of your impure minds, and those who are changed and transformed by the will of the one who is coming will no longer conceive them.

"Rich, you will no longer have terror in debauchery, since for you, debauchery will no longer exist; you, poor, in being ignorant of hunger, will also be ignorant of the banquets that make it fall silent; and all of you will be similar in the scorn, henceforth acquired, of transitory attractions. Your flesh will be distanced from you, your mute senses will be annihilated in a happy forgetfulness, your minds, asleep for centuries, will live extended toward the essential substance, which will be revealed to you, and only the desire to confound yourselves with it will subsist in you."

While he was speaking he listened to muffled plaints coming from every corner of the square, vague at first, gradually swelling, and almost drowning out his words. Without appearing to hear them, he proclaimed more loudly:

"Then you will be similar to those you scorn: to the poets who, with eyes closed and lips muttering, pass close to you without seeing you; to the ascetics who forget the world in the welcoming woods; to all of those, dreamers of illicit dreams—madmen, you say—but who, in spite of your sarcasms, possess the truth."

He stopped; cries of anger dominated his voice. The opulent and the miserable clamored their disappointed hopes; for their particular ambitions, a perennial happiness was insufficient. Since birth, they had desired bitterly to abolish carnal evil by augmenting terrestrial contentment; distant and ideal promises were indifferent to them, and even seemed ironically contemptuous of their present and exceedingly real wishes.

By means of insults and ferocious clamors they expressed their rage; they proclaimed brutally how dissatisfied they were with the aleatory future that was being offered as a lure to those who were demanding enjoyments, or at least the hope of enjoyment, and they asked:

"What is this Messiah that you are announcing coming to do in our midst?"

At a gesture from the herald they fell silent momentarily.

The herald said: "Is there one among you who is crying out in an hour of trouble and appealing to the Elect that he come?"

No one emerged from the mass. They had not called to that one but to another, who would have calmed their appetites and appeased their thirsts by giving them more to eat and drink.

"Let him leave us our feasts," said the rich.

"In spite of their terrors?" asked the man.

"In spite of them."

"We prefer our miseries," cried the poor.

"In spite of their rancor?"

"In spite of them."

"We will be alone in rejoicing," said the rich.

"We might one day equal those who dominate us, and we shall have them under our feet," affirmed the poor.

Then they all extended their fists toward one another. For a moment, forgetful of acts accomplished, thinking uniquely of their eternal and reciprocal hatred, they threatened one another with gestures and voices; but the same thought surged forth at the same instant in their minds, extinguishing their fury momentarily, and they turned toward the envoy of the pontiffs.

"Let the one you have just announced be put to death," they said.

"Is he not the Messiah?" asked the annunciator.

"Let him be put to death, since he is the Messiah," all the people responded.

II

Night had now fallen, putting to sleep the rumor of the city, which forgot, in its satisfied vengeance, the things promised and renounced; and on the slope of a distant hill, darkened by pines shivering under the moon, the savior announced by the diviners and the sibyls was lying, pale and naked. His body was soiled with mud and bruised by the stones with which he had been pelted, but his face was calm, and a pure light bathed him.

Near the Messiah, a young pastor was kneeling, his head bowed, shedding tears. He invoked the victim, he offered his expiatory tears, and, his mouth having touched the forehead of the Elect, he heard a voice resound in the air that soared for a long time over the torpid city, over the mute plain, and he listened, full of an adorable trouble, for the voice said:

"Do not weep; he will live again; always born, always immolated. One day, the purificatory tide of his blood will cover the earth, and, the hour having come, everyone will recognize him."

The Agony of the Spirits

To Stéphane Mallarmé.

The Spirit: "Who calls me?"
Faust: "Terrible vision!"
Goethe.

THE ancient and modern wisdom illuminated the mind of Rabbi Iechiel, and he was a very great, very subtle doctor, expert in the remotest arcana, familiar with the most abstruse ideas. His persuasive words were able to dissipate the most tenacious doubts and vanquish tortuous sophisms. He cured carnal ills by means of simples, and removed the heavy mantle of error by means of the mysterious virtue of the Word.

Abstinence and cilices had purified his soul; and, his will having increased by virtue of his disdain for appearances, he communicated with pure forms and hidden essences. Within the body he perceived the psychic torch; in the universe he attained the matrix of things; in infinite space he approached God. Like a king he marched, dragging behind him the pompous cortege of servile acclamations, followed by the admiration of sages who came to him as to a spring distributing salutary and virtuous waters.

Having recognized that only mystical researches were important, he disdained to awaken germs and create transitory phantoms, although he was able to do so. So he had banished from his dwelling the alembics attesting to puerile alchemies, and the vain crucibles in which gold had slept. The high chamber that his disciples frequented was garnished with manuscripts, grimoires, abraxas stones and strange spheres, and there were symbolic numbers inscribed on the walls.

His life was simple; his nourishment frugal. He excluded meat from his meals for, imbued with Hebraic practices, he feared the blood that the soul had sanctified. In the morning, he wandered through the fields, collecting herbs, rustic healers. When dusk fell, his dwelling filled with pupils anxious for his words; he led them by sure routes to eternal verities, and then, when night came, he accompanied them over the threshold, and meditated until dawn. Whether he slept, no one knew.

One evening, when his disciples were assembled around him, he was talking to them about the Master dearest to his heart, the divine Samian who, having retired to a cave, conquered the supreme realities: Pythagoras the exceedingly wise, who, expelled by the multitudes, came to die voluntarily near the altar of the Muses.[1]

Iechiel commented on the aphorisms that the pious Lysis had conserved and, the living echo of the ancient dead voice, he explained the divine monad, the dyadic created universe that is the immutable being united with changing matter, and the quaternary, the source of imperishable

---

1 The notion that Pythagoras starved himself to death was endorsed by Diogenes Laertius but is contradicted by various biographies concocted by later neo-Platonists, who preferred the thesis that he was murdered.

Nature, clearly. As he had just read the last sentence of the book, he stopped; and then, mechanically he repeated it:

"Thus, when you have abandoned the mortal shells,[1] you will rise into the free air, you will become a god, and for you, Death will lose its power."

A veil had suddenly fallen upon him, enveloping his lucid reason in darkness, and he, who knew how to force the most recalcitrant words to deliver the mysteries they enclosed to him, he, Iechiel, did not understand the meaning hidden beneath those words, limpid as they were: "When you have abandoned *the mortal shells.*" Then, with a gesture, he sent away those who surrounded him and, left alone, he meditated.

The vocables pronounced only had, for him, their sonorous value; he grasped their strict syntax, but they seemed stripped of their virtual qualities, and yet, beneath them, he perceived a symbol all the more grave because he could not bring it to the surface. Why had Pythagoras said "the mortal shells" and not "the mortal shell"?

The rabbi's desire was excited by the pursuit of the problem and, faithful to the precepts of the school, in order to query the abstruse significance, he ripened his senses to the clamor of ambiences. To subdue the flesh, which evokes maleficent phantasms, he observed a rigorous fast; in order to loosen the soul, sometimes rebellious to the solicitations of the dream, he drove away sleep, the progenitor of obscene dreams; and, his intelligence

---

1 The original has *les dépouilles mortelles*, which is, as Iechiel goes on to observe, slightly odd, because *la dépouille mortelle* would normally be translated into English as "mortal remains"; in order to conserve the distinction the story makes between the singular and the plural, I have had to substitute a term facilitating that contrast.

extended toward the unique goal, he absorbed himself in his effort.

One by one, the mirages, the sons of the world that tempt indecisive wills, vanished, and appearances were dissipated. No specious sound resonated in Iechiel's ears; no insidious form conscripted his pupils; he plunged into the luminous air populated by silent, clear undulations emanated by his will.

On the evening of the third day, as the crepuscular gleams appeased once again the assailant rumors, the fugitive waves were immobilized; their curves united in confused lineaments that gradually became more precise, and slowly, the dreamer saw his astral semblance surging forth before him. Like a last reflux, a memory still floated: Iechiel remembered Zoroaster encountering his shade in the gardens of Iran, and without terror, he waited.

The phantom spread its hands toward the one of whom it was born and it spoke. It seemed to the rabbi that the voice emerged from his own mouth, even though it was coming toward him.

"By the power of our evocatory gestures, by the force of constant thoughts, you have expelled me from you, and of your master you have made your slave. For what you want to know, I have come. Interrogate and I will, strictly, tell you the answer. But do not stray into other demands, for I have emerged from the shadow, at your propitious wish, solely to satisfy your pertinent request."

And Iechiel, at the question posed, heard moving in the depths of himself the fateful lines of the sage, of which he had not attained the inclusive comprehension.

"Thus, when you have abandoned the mortal shells, you will rise into the free air, you will become a god, and for you, Death will lose its power."

"Come," said the Spirit, "I shall be your guide. You shall see the Realities, and what will be unveiled before your eyes, only one man has seen: Er, the Armenian, once recalled from Hades."[1]

The rabbi felt his bones distend and his flesh collapse like a rag; the walls seemed to him to open, his pupils dilated, and, through the eyes of his Double, he saw the earth, saddened by its agonies, heavy with the accumulated dead. The clamor of last gasps and the distress of ultimate sighs reached his ears in a tumult of terrors and regrets, which sometimes dominated the tremulous chorus of hopes attained. From recumbent cadavers new forms took flight, imprisoning the souls in a subtler and purer matter, and the forms rose toward the skies, allowing a cover of silence to fall upon the soiled ground, a silence announcing destinies revolved. Iechiel followed them, borne by the Spirit.

A breath was floating, with which the air quivered; it aspired the beings born of unknown lights, which were driven by the intensity of their desire. The ascendant wills awoke, and the hymns latent within them expanded. Iechiel heard the songs:

"Death is not! Let us resuscitate! Toward Wisdom, toward the Torch, toward the supreme Face, toward the splendor of the Uncreated we are going! He is calling us, the thrice Holy Lord! He is attracting us, the One that is. Bless him, the One who was and will be!"

The glorifying syllables purified space; the demons crouched on the threshold of sidereal enclosures fled; very high, in the Orient, ineffable clarities were flamboyant, and the rabbi perceived a voice descending: "In my father's house there are many mansions."

---

1 The story of Er is told in the final section of Plato's *Republic*.

"This is the first," murmured the Spirit. "It is this one that, by the power of his spells, Montanus caused to appear above Pepuza. He named it the celestial Jerusalem."[1]

Before Iechiel, a city loomed up, confused and pale, built with materials unknown to humans. The foundations of the walls were made of a strange, translucent stone of a hyaline hue, through which, at times, eddies of darker tints passed abruptly, like the black clouds that further sadden winter zeniths.

The columns with which the facades were ornamented were sculpted in a particular marble, giving an impression of tempting softness. The rabbi felt himself incited by the fluted shafts that curved inwards at his approach. The avenues that those palaces bordered were prolonged infinitely and faded away in profound mists powdered with gold; they were paved with large slabs, dull and changing in color, which became convex under Iechiel's gaze, and his feet perceived an indefinable sensation as they brushed them, as if he were walking over desiccated roses that had, however, not lost their moisture. Here and there, high towers rose up, whose summits were haloed by violet-tinted figs.

An innumerable crowd animated that city of dream. The beings who composed it belonged to all peoples and all races, but the differences that had characterized

_____

1 Montanus, a second-century Christian convert who claimed inspiration by the Holy Spirit, preached that the New Jerusalem would be established in Pepuza and Tymion in Phrygia. His New Prophecy was condemned by revival sects as a heresy. Tertullian initially defended Montanism but subsequently deserted it. Whether the vision glimpsed here corresponds with Montanist belief is impossible to tell, all the sect's own writings having been destroyed and the hostile attacks that survive being probably slanderous.

them on earth, their anterior habitat, were henceforth less obvious, for Death had delivered them from the grosser molecules most subject to temporary alterations.

Iechiel observed that the others entered with him, having ceased to chant their canticles in passing through the portals, and that, for them, the consciousness of an ascension toward the Immutable had suddenly disappeared. That multitude was agitated as it had been agitated before by ephemeral cycles; similar passions animated it, and although those passions were purified, they had not decreased.

For the second time, the Spirit said to the rabbi: "See!"

Iechiel saw. He saw that dolor was still vivacious, that suffering was perpetuated. However, the agonies of the inhabitants of the immense city were calmer, for the effort to liberate themselves from less rigid bonds was attenuated. Iechiel did not hear the sobs heard previously; the plaints were sublimated; the perception of future happiness being clearer, and the fervor of hopes being magnified by scorn for carnal lures. From those beings that Death, the inevitable sovereign, had struck, other envelopes escaped, jailers of souls, and renascent forces, noisy with rhythms, agitated by propitiatory harmonies, rose toward higher empyreans.

Again, Iechiel followed them.

The air that the attractive powers penetrated was moved by an ejaculatory ecstasy; sonorous waves aggregated in vaporous concerts; whirlwinds variegated with gold developed their melodious spirals; a stellar dust impregnated space. Psalms launched forth:

"By the burden of passions our shoulders are less weighed down, thrice-blessed Lord, thrice-sanctified

Master! Lighter, through the ether that your presence animates, we rise. You who enchain, you who release, in you our hope exalts. Good father, be propitious for us; you who created efficacious repentance, when our miserable marrow had engendered sin; you, holy God, Wisdom, redeem us."

More imperative, the Voice announced:

"In my father's house there are many mansions!"

Again, at the evangelical invocation, the misty silhouettes of a city were outlined.

"The second," stammered the Spirit. "Origen foresaw it."[1]

Through squares and uncertain crossroads, nacreous in a fleecy atmosphere, Iechiel wandered, rediscovering companions taken from neglected regions, companions in whom supreme intelligence, momentarily conquered, was abolished. He mingled with those survivors ignorant of their survival. He rediscovered the ancient anguishes, the fateful despairs, the perpetual terrors, and always triumphant Death, with victorious hands, making new prisons issue from fallen bodies.

To the conquest of more serene altitudes, the rabbi rose.

He went incessantly, in a flight more rapid after each pause, for the flock of the elect, hastier as the oppressive material cover was lightened, drew him along.

The hostile powers attenuated and the enemy sighs vanished. Lustral vibrations permeated the Expanse;

---

1 The prolific second-century ascetic theologian Origen was heavily influenced by neo-Pythagorean thought, which led to his works being condemned as unorthodox and anathematized, but they were not obliterated like Montanist documents. The cosmology of the present story seems to owe something to his ideas but certainly does not reflect them straightforwardly.

rhythmic gleams propagated their spirals; the chanted canticles extended in responses:

"Jut God, to punish us, you made flesh."

"Good God, to redeem us, you made Death."

"Death is the auxiliary of your clemency."

"It is the pledge of your bounty."

In limitless plains the cities flourished, flowers of dream, translucent and white, of a whiteness aggravated by an increasing silence. They received a people of shadows, pale reflections of plastic humans, effaced mirages of incarnations, indecisive persistences of beauties and tresses, obstinations of tears and enfeebled smiles. And those cities multiplied, innumerably, as innumerable as the stellar gems, and the rabbi, in his being, asked:

"How far do they go?"

"To infinity," the Spirit promulgated, "and yet they end, since souls have a goal. Listen to the souls."

Outside their prisons, the souls were reciting prayers. Iechiel could scarcely hear them now; the sound no longer reverberated, it infiltrated, as clay imbibes floodwater:

"You are the Source, we await you. The Unique is in us, we make the Unique. Number is resolved, Genre disappears, the Multiple becomes One. We are born, Death diminishes. We aspire to the Eternal, we are bound for the Absolute."

The fluids irradiated. Flamboyances burst forth in perfumes, were affirmed in melodies; magnetic effluvia vibrated that resolved into aromas, into streaking sparks; vague luminosities accumulated, they expanded into sonorous sheets, they curved into cassolettes instilling cardamoms and myrrhs. Corollas opened, striated with silver, veined with cinnabar; avid pistils moved toward them and they united, sowing pollens that ambered the air.

Soon, Iechiel knew that the last appearances were dissolving. Forms disappeared, impalpable atoms agitated among the persistent clarities. Then, no sudden flash, no importunate scattering came to break the opaline radiant sea; the murmurs and the sounds that subsisted dissolved in the universal respiration and the Invisible alone animated the Ether.

"This is the parvis that you cannot cross," the Spirit attested. "Here, your eyelids must seal your eyes, your ears must close. The essence that is near you will penetrate one day; one day, you will realize the imperishable union. The hour is distant, but it will come. Your bonds are summoning you and summoning me; you have seen; you have heard; your guide in abandoning you."

The Double was resorbed into the rabbi's flesh, and Iechiel awoke, illuminated by the divine breath. He took up the book left with the page open, and slowly, he reread:

"Thus, when you have abandoned the mortal shells, you will rise into the free air, you will become a god, and for you, Death will lose its power."

But from then on, he understood the Word.

Life Without Fear

To F. Vielé-Griffin.[1]

. . . And I fled straight ahead
Blown by the wind of funereal mysteries.
Léon Dierx.

THE traveler had wandered for long days along the banks of the river, the mystical and sovereign river whose waters were still shivering at the memory of divine forms that had bathed there at the dawn of time. He had trodden the sandy and numinous plains in the middle of which the azurine silk of waters spread, and the uncomprehended rumor of waves had lulled his march, sending his weary body to sleep, while their benevolent freshness had reanimated his strength with every dawn.

Perhaps, in chance encounters, he had heard talk of treasures held in the depths of virgin forests by the vigilant ferocity of dwarfs, inflexible custodians of gems committed to their guard, and he was going to their dangerous conquest without his heart failing. The tacit complicity

---

1 Francis Vielé-Griffin (1864–1937) was an American-born Symbolist, a close associate of Mallarmé and one-time schoolfellow of Henri de Régnier.

of the desert encouraged his dreams, which no unusual sound came to disturb, for the song of the regal waves spread mysterious vibrations through the air, auxiliaries to his thoughts.

One morning, the bitter breath of the warm, dry wind of the solitudes fell silent; a breeze freshened by tender aromas enlaced the traveler, the caress of warm fingers brushed his forehead, and he saw the lotus flowers of the river open their calm eyes wider. He sensed that the woods were close, and he hastened toward the Occident, guided by the sun. Gradually, the odors became more precise, brutal myrrhs, bright sandalwoods, explosive fragrances; toward evening, all the balms of the atmosphere were gushing from invisible cassolettes, and the Star, at its nadir, was veiled with yellow vapors, like a golden censer misted by emanated perfumes.

The limpid horizon was obscured, violet fabrics swayed, agitated by unknown breaths; they darkened, a blue mass appeared, which suddenly broke up, allowing the sight of yellow holes of light, and, like a distant moving flock, the forest surged forth, distinctly, its oaks rearing up, attempting the skies, where the aligned swathes of the clouds still lay.

Then, abruptly, night fell, perfumed with stars; the vision, momentarily manifest, folded back into the shadow, and the traveler lay down to sleep, for he dared not violate the slumber of the thickets.

When he awoke, he prostrated himself, in order to render the sylvan gods favorable, and penetrated beneath the vessel of enlaced branches. No path tore with its amicable meanders the ground oppressed by the secular humus of fallen leaves, imbricated like bronze scales. The man, interrogating the indicative ferns, plunged into the undergrowth.

He marched for a long time, inattentive to the murmurs of the foliage, the appeal of gushing springs, the invitations of lakes whose pupils palpitated in the centers of clearings, the solicitations of cooing pigeons and the flight of fallow deer breaking through the thickets. He advanced, solely concerned with the goal; sometimes, stirred by initial covetousness, he parted the brambles, under which his anxious eye thought it had perceived the ocellus of a gem or the gleam of metal; then, disappointed, he whipped the brushwood with his bloody hand and resumed his route.

Around him the forest became denser, mingling its branches, combining its crowns, reinforcing the arrogant domes of its foliage, beneath which nothing but a diffuse light any longer penetrated. An armed captive, the trees, jealous guardians of the shadow, pressed him. Their trunks rose up, like a wall, to silence, broken at intervals by the grating skeleton of a dead warrior, extending his denuded arms and whitened by the excreta of birds of prey.

The immobility of the mantle of verdure aggravated the wild majesty of the wood, and the traveler marched beneath a tideless sea. His mind, haunted by chimeras, populated the leaden ocean that oppressed his cranium with monsters, and when a ray of light pierced the somber network momentarily, he thought he saw the bellies of fabulous fish glinting.

Incessantly, he went on, drinking dormant water from hollows in rocks, eating bitter berries that crowned the bushes, ignoring his lassitude henceforth, for his skin was tanned and his feet were hardened. Sometimes, however, when the darkness increased, he sat down on a fallen tree-trunk and went to sleep.

One evening, perhaps desirous of an instant of forgetfulness, he let himself fall, but got up again abruptly;
instead of the customary ligneous couch, he felt beneath
him the cold of marble, and he looked around. The earth
was strewn with fallen columns; half-buried frontons
emerged here and there, cippi rose up garlanded with
moss, deflowered capitals hid under the foliage, a rusty
plowshare abandoned on a stone seemed to be guarding
the threshold of an abolished palace.

Among the vestiges of the dead city the man wandered.
His profound melancholy harmonized with the widowed
pedestals, the debris of triumphal arches frustrated of
antique glories, fallen statues, anonymous witnesses of
heroic gestures, time having corroded their faces, and
broken stumps whose grooves oozed tears, evocative of
prodigious mourning.

The further the traveler advanced, the more the ruins
accumulated. There were now porticos deprived of their
friezes, which displayed down below the prancing horses
and the files of suppliant soldiers; pylons with winged
spheres at the summit; hypetral temples—the bronze
sheets of the roofs were broken—which exposed gods
swept by iconoclastic rains, and basins of red porphyry
that bristled with the lances of aquatic plants.

Gradually, the obscurity was also attenuated as the bushy
giants became less dense; hyaline rays furrowed the green
thickness and were displayed in pale patches on the mossy
metopes and marmoreal acanthi. The scattered debris
thinned out; roads designed their duller ribbons; wheels
leaned over with broken rims, incrusted with grooves; neglected pikes drove their points into the sides of stagnant
ditches; aqueducts aligned their channels through beeches;
and suddenly, in the distance, a city appeared.

The man made haste, and entered it through a gate whose battens were disjointed. No dog spiteful to vagabonds saluted him with barking or threats, and the conqueror of the mystic jewels felt his heart beat faster at the mysterious aspect of the hatching dream. Like a king whose renown terrifies, and who sees frightened people fleeing his presence as he pillages their dwellings, he entered the deserted outlying districts. Cracked houses with caved-in roofs and vacillating walls bordered the empty streets; the perrons with shaky steps seemed to have forgotten familiar feet; the paths of adjacent gardens disappeared under hectic grass and the wisterias of arbors swung their clusters over sculpted benches devoid of the couples of yore.

In spite of the widowhood of things, however, the traveler sensed hostile presences behind the sad stones, and he waited at crossroads where fountains murmured for beings that finally came.

He saw them advancing, clad in faded fabrics, and their slow and weary step evoked imprisoned shades retained in the places they had once loved. He approached; his fingers brushed the cloak of a woman whose blonde hair spread over the glaucous tissue enveloping her shoulders, but the woman, without a shudder and without a glance, drew away. The traveler hesitated; perhaps, in order to follow her, he was waiting for a gesture of surprise or interrogation. But the woman, indifferent, did not turn round toward the man, who had been unable to see her eyes.

The phantasmal inhabitants were still passing in front of the man, and none appeared to perceive his unusual advent. He mingled with groups in order to listen for spoken words, but the mouths remained obstinately closed and he understood, vaguely, that the walkers were silent not in order to avoid indiscreet requests but by virtue of an inability to speak. Fear gripped him; he wanted to hear a voice, even his own, that might be able to break the charm and extract those vain forms from their fateful torpor.

A child stopped and, leaning against a stele, remained motionless; the folds of his robe agitated around his legs, which no shiver stirred. The traveler placed his hand on the inclined head and interrogated the child. The dormant echoes awoke and propagated the spoken syllables in infinite vibrations; the child did not reply. The traveler lifted up the inclined face and recoiled, terrified.

He had seen the eyes: two very large eyes whose sharp lashes seemed never to have been lowered; profound eyes ignorant of the veil of eyelids; large dull eyes that had no gaze; empty eyes that reflected the trees and the sky, horrible and placid mirrors insensible to frissons of joy and the wrinkles of dolor; the impassive eyes of a blind person who saw.

A nameless fear gripped the man. Certainly, the stagnancy of nocturnal pools in which the moon itself trembles, the agony of drops of water in the calices of poisonous flowers, the sticky crystal with which an octopus fascinates its victim, had stirred him with an unspeakable terror, but at that moment, before the unexpected death of those living eyes, his flesh dissolved in anguish, the breath of the inexplicable stirred his bones and he felt the terror of the unknown.

Then, frightened, he pushed the child away, who collapsed on the ground, as a passive marble collapses, and he fled. Stumbling over the paving stones of the street, bumping into the insensible automata whose crowd had grown, he fled, clutching at the flowery velvet of capes, and his emotion requested the vivacious forest he had quit.

Out of breath, his knees weakening and his legs buckling, he stopped in a vast square ornamented with colonnades of twisted pillars; in the middle, alone, an old man was crouched. The traveler looked at him for a long time; the presence of the solitary individual reassured his demented mind, and simultaneously awakened fraternal emotions within him. The sudden tranquility that calmed him had not deceived him; he recognized a fellow, and slowly, he said: "A man!"

At that exclamation the old man raised his head and said: "What are you doing here, violator, and what sordid research authorizes you to profane the city where the illusory sonorities are dead? Why do you trouble my dream, which populates these fallen palaces and porticos with its unique palpitation? Go away; you have lost the route that leads to desired treasures."

"Most wise," replied the traveler, "answer the question that I am going to pose to you, and you will liberate my soul from malign troubles. Then, perhaps, I can go away reassured."

"Speak, in order that I can drive away your importunate presence by my response."

"Tell me, ascetic, who are the people who are wandering the morose streets? What punishment or what will has rendered them thus?"

"Listen; you will learn the wrath of offended gods and the power of the elect they love. Here rose a proud city of merchants and scribes, a city from which consoling rhythms and noble harmonies were banished, a city of abject mimes and lascivious ballerinas, a city of carnal joys and cupid desires. Clad in crimson and gold, constellated with sumptuous and heavy jewels, the inhabitants rejoiced in the death of the aedes, and in their feasts they promulgated the inanity of supreme essences; they had even erected a basalt obelisk, and on that obscene symbol they had written that Mystery was not.

"One day, a hermit magnified by mysterious austerities penetrated this city as you have penetrated it. Gravely, he came to sit down at the banquets of the rich, and he remonstrated with guests wreathed with fresh corollas. At first they listened with indulgent smiles; then, made anxious by his speeches, which might have awakened torpid beliefs and reanimated deadly aspirations in the depths of certain souls, they chased away the hermit, and the children of the poor pursued him with trenchant stones. Then, before going through the gates, the man they were expelling turned to them and said:

"'Listen to me, blasphemers! Laugh again around laden tables, laugh beside abominable beds; laugh freely, for now you shall no longer know fear.'

"They laughed, the fools, glad to have conquered peace. From that day on they did not know nocturnal terrors: the sharp and delicious frisson that falls from the sky on moonless night, the sweet tremor experienced on the edge of lakes enameled by the calices of white lotuses, like the navels of virgins. They no longer knew the divine dread born of sumptuous forests, nor the tender anguish near flowers sobbing at dusk, nor the dolorous emotion that the wind propagates from dusk to dawn; they no longer knew Fear, the father of subtle joys. Even banal emotion no longer brushed their hearts, and the agitation of the gambler anxious that he might lose disappeared, along with the apprehension of the merchant thinking of distant fleets menaced by the sea, the disquiet of the debauchee recalling possible maladies, a recollection once exciting, and the secret terror that renders blasphemy ineffable. With fear fled all delight, all curiosity, all temptation, and henceforth, no will shook the torpor of blunted senses.

"You have seen, have you not, those merchants and scribes, and their icy pupils have frightened your reason? You questioned them and they did not reply; indifference has veiled their eyes and blocked their ears. They still procreate, not for satisfaction or out of duty, but in order that the malediction of the holy man they offended should be perpetuated and in order that their descendants can, for a long time yet, terrify the intruders who come toward them, like you. And I, seeking solitude and silence, have quit the woods where too many tumultuous existences seethe, and have found refuge where my thought can collect itself without anything troubling it, since I no longer live in the midst of the living. Leave me alone, then, stranger; your hostile breath is dispersing my visions."

The traveler bowed to the disdainful old man, and resumed his route, guided by the green summits that still unfurled on the horizon.

The Flowers

To Stuart Merrill.[1]

And I gazed into the depths of the placid lake.
Shelley.

FOR weeks, months and years, the enemy army had invested the city that the valor of intrepid captains defended. Then, one morning, the besieged troops were defeated, decimated by multiplied assaults and fruitless sorties and weakened by privations. In spite of the fabulous heroisms, devotions and superhuman sacrifices, the walls had fallen under the shock of irresistible battering rams, and, the breach having been made, the hostile cohorts had invaded the ramparts. The wielders of slings

---

1 Stuart Merrill (1863–1915) was the son of an American diplomat posted to Paris in 1866, where he completed his education, with Pierre Quillard and René Ghil as classmates, and became an associate of Mallarmé before returning to the USA in 1884. Most of his work was written in French and published in Paris, but his only American publication, a collection of translations of French prose-poems, *Pastels in Prose* (1890) became an important document introducing the Symbolists to the English language. He returned to live in Paris in 1890; like the majority of his French associates he became an Anarchist, which did not go down well in his homeland and led to his being disinherited by his father.

and the archers, henceforth masters of the towers, had rained their stones and arrows upon the crowds, and the following day, the hoplites and pikemen had spread out through the streets of the city, shaken by the horses of heavy cataphractarii.

Rendered impatient by their long wait, the invaders rushed forward with furious cries in the exasperated desire for gold, murder and palpitating women. To preserve their familiar gods, which the priests removed far from the carnage, the virgins had descended on to the thresholds and, pale in long white bridal garments, they had offered the agonizing lilies of their flesh to the lust of soldiers maddened by long continence. Soon, in the blood of defunct maidenheads, the young women were gasping, mingling their terrors with dominating spasms; soon they died on the thresholds, chosen altars, and even death did not liberate them from inexorable embraces.

Night put a stop to the evil work; the sky was covered by a silent pack of black clouds, and the peace of darkness prostrated the sated males on the ground.

The bloody dawn of battles extended its simarre over the bleak palaces and over the city reminiscent of a garden mourning the death of candid rose-bushes. The scattering of flowered bodies made the pavements of crossroads and squares pale, and the priests who followed the conquerors cried in horror at the sacrilege. Their purifying processions moved through the streets and the porticos, and the harsh militiamen mingled their repentant voices with the chants of the hierodules who were warding off avenging calamities by means of their incantations.

Pyres of sandalwood impregnated with propitious balms burned all day, penetrating the air with lustral emanations, preparing for the expiatory rites, and the vigil for the dead was made by the most valiant leaders, who, wreathed by their weapons, remained prostrated all night, while the cavaliers of the sacred lesions sounded in bronze buccinas the glory of the immolated and the remorse of the murderers.

The next day, the virgins were placed on stretchers florid with scabious; they had been decorated with necklaces of amethysts, and each of them bore on the forehead an opal whose cold ocellus was open. They were carried between the cinerary braziers outside the ramparts, and the cortege headed toward a consecrated lake that the priests had chosen. There the cadavers were laden with heavy gold chains, and then the benevolent hands of eunuchs buried them in the waters, which opened up with mysterious welcoming sounds.

In the evening, the devastators burned the city, and, by the light of the colossal torch that launched hectic flames toward the stars, they drew away, carrying with them the sumptuous booty that was heaped up on the carts.

When the last standards, alone, were perceptible in the distance, fluttering on the horizon like birds with sparkling plumage, the vanquished came down from the hills where, hidden among the oaks, they had witnessed the rapes and the supreme conflagration. On the blackened columns and the broken battens of bronze doors, they sat down in groaning despair, and the tacit dolor of abolished marble harmonized with their anguish.

They wept over the insulted gods, the powerful reduced to flight, like helpless children carried away by their nurses; they wept over the looted hearths, deprived of their cherished jewels and atavistic riches, of which destiny had frustrated the heirs; but when they thought about the beautiful virgins who had made the offering of their first fruits, dying without knowing chosen amour, the clamor of their sobs spread the mourning of their souls over the plain, all the way to the nearby woods.

The memory of evenings when tender conversations and furtive confessions had been scattered along the paths penetrated the ephebes with an irreparable sadness, and their hearts, empty henceforth, clamored with futile appeals.

O amicable woods populated by attentive couples, only the violet mists of twilight will come now to recall the former presences; only the faithful echoes will repeat the syllables once heard; but the mirrors of springs will no longer reflect beloved faces, and the deflowered garlands hung from rustic cippi devoted to the goddess will perpetuate the regrets by their testimony.

Now, a venerated ascetic who had accompanied the funerals came to the young men and offered to take them to those buried in the tomb of the waters by the repentant violators. They followed him along the roads scarred by the wheels of the war-carts.

Here and there, in the hollows of ruts, lay precious objects dropped by the predators, whom the heaped-up spoils had doubtless rendered inattentive; there were gem-studded monstrances, caskets with emerald stria, amulets ornamented with inestimable jewels. But the feet of the widowed lovers collided indifferently with the caskets, the monstrances and the amulets, and none of them could be gladdened by the abandonment of things, for the flood of salty tears drowned their eyes, and the claw of coughing fits clutched their breasts.

On a mound overlooking the lake the guide stopped, while the desolate descended toward the shores denuded of reeds. They lay down on the ground and, their foreheads leaning over, they brushed the cold metal of the waters. Some, immobile, their eyelids closed, appeared to be listening to illusory voices; others dilated their haggard eyes, trying to pierce the glaucous densities that detained the polluted and ravaged bodies; some implored the dead, speaking to them as before, pausing to hear the responses that resonated within them and then resuming the imaginary dialogue; and some, less modest, heaped the heavens with insults and threats, exhausting their chagrin in convulsive movements.

Standing on the hill, the noble ascetic clad in his woolen robe extended his hands over the funerary waters, spreading benedictions, invoking the gods that the devotees had preserved from insults.

"Very great," he said, "let your power be manifest in honor of the pure maidservants devoted to your temples. When frightened, in the arms of our priests, you requested protective shelter, they went toward the assailing hordes, and their frail breasts were preservative for you, more than the outdated ramparts. Fearless, you knew the fear of insults that were spared you by the meek loins offered; manifest your glory and your clemency; resurrect the chaste who died to save you."

With the ascetic's prayers, the ephebes mingled the chorus of their supplications. Suddenly, on the surface of the lake, like a thousand jetting springs, drops of blood surged forth. They spread out, crimson leaves issued from invisible plants, and those leaves were streaked with veins; they grew, and from them, flowers were born, illuminating the air with their strange splendors: calices whose nacre evoked the absent flesh, hyaline corollas whose perfume was reminiscent of the vanished balms.

They were alive, the supernatural flowers; their pistils capped with gold rose up and their stems, proud or softly flexible, agitated like lovers' arms. They reminded the supplicants of the attitudes and gestures of yore, for their new plasticity had kept the reflection of departed forms. In the carmine of petals, the young men rediscovered the smiles of old, and even the droplets that trembled on the flesh of calices and on the green tunics seemed to them to be the tears that the lovers had wept before the profaning warriors.

Then, still kneeling, they called to them, uttering insistently the cherished names of the resuscitated, and the flowers moved in response to the words heard. Slowly, modestly, lowering their stems like the necks of swans, they advanced, undulating and supple, toward the ecstatic adorers.

Many, driven by their impatient tenderness, went into the water, and those the flowers seized, dragging them swooning and enraptured into the depths of the nuptial lake; others extended their hands, which the flowers came to join, they implored them, and on their bosoms they grew, multiplying, intoxicating them with ineffable odors, filling their heads with vibrations of amour; but in the fingers of some, the flowers withered, morose and desiccated, and all of those fled into the countryside, keeping the treasure acquired or lamenting the hope deceived.

Alone, beside the newly impassive waters, the solitary individual remained, nobly clad in his woolen robe, distributing his benedictions, thanking the gods whom the pure and the chaste devotees, who had died to save them, had preserved from insult.

The Incarnations

To A. Rouf.[1]

What do you know of the absolute?
Why is it not coming to me?

> The Gnosis.

ALONE in that Levantine city filled with a varied crowd of strangers I was wandering through the noisy streets at the hour when, the sun having fled, the relative coolness of the air invites the inhabitants to come outside. As the clash of colors variegating the fabrics, the smoky tints in which the houses were clad, the uniform smalt of the sky and even the somber mirror of the sea, stained here and there by white sail, no longer solicited my gaze, requested too many times by that spectacle, I came to sit down before the door of one of the little cafés where the silent clients were smoking, while the perfume of the mocha that filled the cups mingled with the aromatic puffs of the exhaled tobacco.

Seated, I lit the chibouk that a young waiter of equivocal allure presented to me, and confined myself to dreams

---

1 This dedication is enigmatic, but in view of the story's setting it might refer to someone of that name from the Near East that Lazare met in Paris.

stirred up by the blonde floating gauze of the Latakia. An abrupt shock of voices, doubtless the tumult of a quarrel, woke me up, and my eyes, previously distracted, made enquiries of my neighbors of hazard. Rapidly, I judged them to be indifferent, all amorphous in physiognomy and anonymous in attitude: Armenians with conical bonnets, Arabs enshrouded in white gandourahs, bombastic Turks with the cranium topped by a red fez. Cursing my vanished dream, difficult to recapture, I was about to get up when the advent of a strange individual retained me.

He was a Chinaman, whom nothing in his attire distinguished from his compatriots, at least at first glance; he was clad, according to the Celestial custom, in a dark-hued robe ornamented with blue silk, and was coiffed in a shiny black cap. However, even though he wore that costume with the ease of a natal habit, his nationality appeared dubious to me, for certain features of his visage differentiated him clearly from the ordinary subjects of the Son of Heaven. His complexion, bistre rather than yellow, his eyes deprived of a canthus, and his fleshy red lips attested a non-Mongolian race and attached him to a divergent ethnic type.

The form of his nose was a revelation to me, however; it was long, curved, holed by wide, mobile nostrils and, in accordance with contradictory opinions, laudatory or denigratory, might have been described as a nose like an eagle's beak, or a nose like a vulture's beak. The memory was invoked in me of old reading, and I remembered Père Gozani's letter recounting how he had found a few Jewish families in Cai-fum-fou, who had come to China, according to him, before the birth of Jesus.[1]

1 The letter cited was written by the Jesuit Jean-Paul Gozani in 1704 to his superior, reporting a visit he made to a Jewish community in

I examined my singular neighbor again, and soon ceased to doubt that I had before me one of those Hebrews who prided themselves, probably for diplomatic reasons, on not having shed the blood of the redeemer and making a title of glory of that forbearance, due in reality to the hazard of an anterior emigration that had made it geographically impossible for them to act as their brethren had. That particularity aggravated the curiosity that drove me to acquaint myself with the Celestial Jew with whom I was rubbing shoulders.

A benevolent incident furnished me with an opportunity to do so: the Jew sneezed. I saluted him with the Hebraic formula requisite in that circumstance and, after having sneezed again, perhaps to solicit a further misheard benediction, which I generously gave him, he said to me: "You're an Israelite?"

"Yes," I replied, "and you too, doubtless."

"I am, but schismatic, like all my compatriots."

"Schismatic?" I said. "Do you not worship the only Jehovah?"

"Yes," he replied, "although we call him indifferently Tien, Cham-Tien and Hotoi, but we also honor Confucius, who was very wise, and our venerable ancestors who evoked God. Nevertheless, in order not to hide anything from you, I ought to tell you that, for many years, I have no longer practiced the religion in question, whose metaphysics seems insufficient to me."

---

what is nowadays known as Kaifeng. The details of the account the Chinese Jew gives of his beliefs in this story are derived from the letter. The Synagogue of Kaifeng had been visited by previous travelers, and Gozani was not the first missionary sent to investigate it, but his account became the best known.

"Are you in quest of a Divinity more admissible than the burning bush of Horeb?"

"No. I have formed cosmological and philosophical ideas regarding the universe, humankind and the supreme essence whose ensemble satisfies my speculative needs well enough. I only quit China moved by the very natural desire to know my coreligionists scattered to the four corners of the world."

"Would it be unwelcome for me to ask you your opinion of those you have seen?"

"Not at all, and although you belong to them, I hope not to be unwelcome in responding to you that my opinion is not entirely favorable."

I attested my indifferent independence and he continued.

"I have found that race, which is renowned everywhere for its unbreakable unity, more multiple than any other of those that impose themselves upon or insinuate themselves into foreign lands. I have seen that race, which mysterious destinies once seemed to promise august glories, dominated by the basest preoccupations. The ears of those men are closed to the voices of those who would like to bring them back to the road on which Sinai fulgurated and where the vaticinations of the Nabis resounded. They have lain down at the foot of the pedestal where the beast that Moses cast down stands once again; even the mediocre belief that once attached them to the suprasensible has vanished, and henceforth, their brains are only full of the harmful smoke of transitory vanities."

"Alas, how right you are! It is only too true that the princes of those disaggregated tribes oppress, with a practical scorn, the rare individuals among them disposed to escape toward more spiritual regions. To tell the truth, also

the majority of Christians by whom they are surrounded
do not appear to me to be motivated by nobler aspirations,
but the most serious grievance I have against the Jews, my
brothers, is not the general grievance that I have against
all humankind."

"What is it, then?"

"I reproach that people for an unfortunate inconsequence, a manifest contradiction, which consists of bitterly
rejecting the realization of ideas that were its directors in
all times."

"Explain what you mean."

"That's easy. Is it not that people who, at their origin,
from the day when the Cherub expelled them from Eden,
foresaw, announced and hoped imperturbably for the
Messiah? And is it not that people who rejected the son of
man who came to confirm the prophecies of the inspired
long-beards who had proclaimed them in the streets of
Jerusalem, in the roads of Babylon and the outskirts of
Nineveh, in the midst of calamities and triumphs, in exile
and in torments, under the teeth of saws and the bites of
wild beasts? And, that man having died who wanted to
redeem them, did they not also mistake the successors,
perhaps the elect, of the carpenter: Alroy or Serenus,
Julian or Zachariah, Sabbatai or Onias?"[1]

"What you call inconsequence, appears to me to be a
fatal logic. Is it not better, and above all more indulgent,
to believe that if the Jews have not, until now, welcomed

---

1 This list includes three well-known Messiah claimants, the eighth-
century Syrian Christian Serene, or Serenus; the twelfth-century Persian Alrui, or David Alroy and the seventeenth-century Ottoman Jew
Sabbatai Zevi. Julian is presumably the Roman Emperor called Julian
the Apostate by Christians, and Zachariah the Biblical prophet. Onias
was the name of a dynasty of high priests during the era of the Second Temple.

the Redeemer, it is because it was impossible for them to recognize him as such?"

"Why?"

Because Theudas, Barkokebas or Jesus manifested themselves in forms and with tendencies inaccessible to the common run of Hebrews.[1] There are two messianic currents in Israel, just as there are two categories of well-entrenched mind. On the one hand, the prophetic current, characterized by the grim hatred of the rich and oppressors, represented by those who expect of the Anointed a justice mild to the humble, to the wretched shepherds of Juda, to weak Galilean fishermen; on the other hand, that same belief, transformed by the dense brain of opulent and hardened Pharisees, brothers of Sidonians and Carthaginians. Those merchants made a model of the Elect so different from the one given by Daniel that they could not recognize the terrestrial monarch of whom they dreamed in the pitiful Nazarene, who marched followed by a cortege of publicans, fallen women and soothed lepers."

"I understand. Those hardened individuals, as you put it, will only salute the Liberator when he consents to clothe himself in an appearance adequate to the idea that they have made of him."

"That's what I think."

"I fear, then, that until the *consummatum est* of centuries, the Jews, and many others, will cling to their error, for God will not be able to diminish."

---

1 Theudas was a Jewish rebel in the first century A.D., described as a charlatan by Josephus, and also mentioned, anachronistically, in the *Acts of the Apostles*. Simon bar Kokhba, also known as Barkokebas or Barchochebas led a similar revolt, temporarily successful, in the second century A.D.; the sage Rabbi Akiva suggested that he might be the Messiah.

"Undoubtedly, but out of humility he can lower himself. Has he not already done so?"

"Who can tell?"

"Listen to what was told to me in India, where the illustrious kingdom of Kranganore was once founded by Hebrew emigrants,[1] by an old rabbi deeply imbued with the principles of the Kabbala and favored by God with special revelations. For several days we had long conversations together, all essential and profound in meaning. I had scarcely quit Cai-fum-fou, so he had a great deal to teach me, and he instructed me in the esotericism of the Mosaic faith, speculating about the names of the forty-two letters, searching everywhere for the Trinity that, according to him, sustains the universe. He found it in the phylacteries, in the three times of the daily hymn, in the letter *shin*, and above all in the vocable Yahveh, which only the high priest uttered ten times a year, at the expiatory feast.

"One evening, in the grotto in which he made his dwelling, we talked about the destinies promised to the nations. 'Because of the triple essence,' he told me, 'God ought to incarnate himself three times in the bosom of the people he has chosen. The principle of love has come; the principle of wisdom will soon come; and finally the generative force that will transform both of them and render them comprehensible to all, for it will be produced under a clear veil and will be affirmed divested of alarming attributes, or even discouraging virtues.'

"When he had spoken those words he was resorbed in a silence that was soon broken by the flow of annunciatory

---

1 The tradition of the Malabar Jews contends that the port known in English as Cranganore, now Kodungallu, was founded by Jewish immigrants.

visions. His eyes were illuminated by unknown gleams, his entire body quivered, agitated by the divinatory breath, and he spoke in a voice that was no longer his own, a voice stirred by the echo of another:

"'Once, Israel had planted his tents on the patrimony of dispossessed Canaan. By means of the sword, by cunning and divine aid, he had established his kingdom near the banks of the Jordan and close to the mount of lies, he had build the holy city, the center of the world, the mother of destinies, the sacred torch whose glare illuminated the world: Sion, which magnified the temple of the Unique and the Triple; Sion, which desiccated the loquacity of doctors, polluted the altars of Kamosch, the wooded heights of Aschera; Sion, city of scribes, refuge of prophets; Sion, palace of kings and dwelling of warriors; Sion, market of the rich and refuge of pastors.

"'She, the mystic Queen, misunderstood the remonstrations of her true son; the defeats, the shame and the captivity itself did not unseal her eyes, which the vapor of bad sacrifices had obscured. She was the prostitute seated on the far side of ditches, waiting on the roads, only offering the garden of her delights to those who covered her miserable belly with a mantle of gold striped with gems, and rejecting the pastors clad in coarse skins who asked her for a maternal kiss. One day you came to her, son of David presaged by a thousand mouths, foreseen by the sibyls, saluted by the seers, and your daughter turned away from you, soiled your face and lacerated your limbs. You let the blood flow that the lance provoked, and was summoned by the thorns and the nails, the candid blood that wanted to save you. Your father made the wind of his anger blow, the wind that broke Sion's tiara, the wind that dispersed the predestined children.'

"The voice changed then; its accents became shriller, penetrating me like piercing blades, and the stiff hand of the rabbi reached out, unveiling the shadow in which all things lay.

"'Under the burden of sin, Israel had fled as the scapegoat of old fled, expelled from the sanctuary, obsessed with the crimes of which the tribes lightened themselves, pursued by invincible anger. Israel fled as Cain had fled, as Samiri had fled, as Ahasuerus had fled, those accused ones who were its soul. Every drop of ineffable blood, for which they took responsibility on behalf of their posterity, they paid for in insults and spittle, and for the anguished sweat they paid in anguished sweat, and they drank from the chalice for long years, for very long years.'

"Again the voice mutated; it sounded bitter and mocking, sniggering ironically.

"'Adonai, however, who had always had an inexplicable affection for his people, extended his law over them. He had extracted them from the ramparts of Assyria, he broke the chains that confined the old ghettos, he appeased the fury of conquering nations, he assigned a center once again to the glory of the Hebrews, recalled from the confines of the world. Strengthened by centuries of oppression, hungry for restrictive justice acting in its favor, Israel dominated, triumphed, and now it is once again the terrestrial lever; its foot is on the neck of kings. Sion shudders in her entrails; she awakes like the child palpitating in its mother's womb; she emerges from ancient ruins and soon, rebuilt, she will guide peoples and sovereigns.

"'I see her again, modern and beautiful, erecting her ingenious towers, her frivolous and sumptuous towers. Again she fills with the same merchants and the same scribes, and the descendants of the pastors groan under a more rigorous yoke. They are the serfs henceforth, those who toil for their masters, who weave the purple that they will not wear, and string the pearls that will never ornament their foreheads; they go in search, over distant seas, of the sumptuous foodstuffs of which their mouths will be frustrated, and they will beg for the bread that their fingers knead.'

"The voice became exaggerated, mockingly dolorous.

"'The smoke of their sins certainly obsesses their God, that redoubtable Adonai who alternately awakens and puts to sleep his anger. As once before, pity grips him, he interrogates that race again, perhaps ripe for its destiny, again he wants to reveal the truth to it. But the son is wearied by his unfortunate advent and the blasphemies that cover him in thousands of centuries past; is not love inaccessible to those who hate? Like the father, he abandons them; perhaps wisdom will bring the impure back to the primitive sheepfolds?

"'The Spirit comes that obscure mages had announced, and, doubtless to mock the doctors, it is weighed down in the body of a woman, the body of a woman that all believe they have possessed, a woman soiled by all the obscene rituals. But if people regard her equivocally, that is rather due to her sex than the divine mission with which she is invested, and in which no one believes. Sad wretches in rags follow her footsteps, and while the tender and profound parables that she spreads at crossroads and squares are mocked, the leaven of iniquities ferments in the heart of her disciples and the powerful tremble under unleashed hatreds.'

"The rabbi stood up, haggard, his eyes veiled by tears.

"'Love had not been heard; wisdom was unable to vanquish. I see the hill and the antique torture restored.

"'The lance has resurfaced, the priests are weaving the crown of thorns, the rods are brandished, the nails exhumed, the adorable wood raised up, the blood springs forth again, impotent to save; the victim agonizes, she dies, the earth shakes, the skies darken and the executioners flee, frightened.

"'Israel, detestable race, witness to and murderer of God, once more you are chastised. The city of your pride falls in ruins, the temple of your lies crumbles, the kings that you tamed raise their heads again, your subjects, strong in the precepts that the Spirit teaches, abandon you. Like the wheat that the sower dispenses on arid ground, and whose seeds the wind blows away, you will groan on foreign soils. You will bend your superb neck, you will accept outrages, punished but not penitent, and standing on pyres, extended on the wheel of torture, you will confess the God that you do not understand.'

"Exhausted, the rabbi let himself fall on to the carpet of leaves, and then resumed bitterly:

"'Juda is vanquished, the earth awakes, guided by Wisdom, the daughter of God, born of a virgin resuscitated in order to conceive. But you have invincible attractions for Adonai, eternal horde that rejected Mizraim. Grim Sabaoth, you who massacred Moab, Edom and Assur pitilessly, you cannot see your favorite children in the vale of tears for long. Can their sobs move your heart uniquely, then, father of all? You bring them out of servitude; they pullulate, they invade, their hands hold empires, the gold captive of their cunning groans, and in base prisons the progenitor sun they have conquered weeps. Jerusalem, here you are again, victorious over abysms! Dear princess of hopes, you have recovered the opals of your triple diadem; you are seated amid the privets of beloved gardens and the laurels that sense your breath shiver. Pure Queen with the profaned bosom, who protects the humble and subjugates the haughty, you are splendid with all beauties, pale with all sadnesses.'

"Now the words are emerging from the mouth of the seer in a hiss; they perforate my skull.

"'Who retains the rich in their cupidity? Forgiveness is granted to them for every fault; the treasure of indulgences ripens for them alone. In the glare of divine wrath, they hear future forbearance, they authorize themselves final immunities. Good livestock of Liban, give your wool, shear yourself, you will go forth stark naked, confident in creative mercy; gentle artisan, construct royal beds, the earth will be your couch, and cold will sap you of the strength of rancor; mournful laborer, make the wheat germinate, and you shall nourish yourself on the tares; women emaciated by fasting will procreate daughters, and they will divert the ennui of the predators; engender sons, and they will defend the merchants and the scribes.

"'You are saddened, O Adonai, by the demands of your faithful; you dream in your Heaven, which discontents the people of your dilection. You showed them good; however, they never saw it. You said to them: *Here is the right road*; they did not hear you. You cried out to them: *Go naked in order to grasp paradise again*; they jeered, and went forth enveloped in constellated brocade. Are you going to warn them again, to shake the audacious tree to see whether the fruits will fall that will form your clemency?

If you remain silent, if the thunder becomes mute, if the lightning no longer frightens in lacerating the clouds, if the impetuous clouds no longer summon deluges, if plagues no longer announce your name, they will believe the Ether uninhabited, and the lords of opulence will nourish themselves henceforth on the flesh of plebs, certain of being unpunished. Hear the wretches who are clamoring to you: *The sword is extinct that the Archangel held; the mist of forgetfulness hides Eden.*

"'The Son veils his face and his loving heart weeps. The Spirit has turned his head and his heart of wisdom has given up. You come, Father, regenerative power, you descend.

"'What abject form have you chosen, most skillful? What sordid appearance have you adopted, connoisseur of souls? Is that you, breath of Carmel, voice of Moria, flame of Sedom? Have you denied Beauty, since it has been insulted; have you abdicated Charm and Mildness, since they have been expelled?'

"The rabbi leaned toward me, and his index finger pointed into space.

"'Can you see, in the city adorned with all the luxuries, the hideous little Jew with dirty yellow hair, the gummed-up eyes, the twisted mouth and the hirsute beard? He emerges from shady houses and whispers words to the prepubescent who pass by; he preaches evil, and people listen to him, seduced. The sight of him does not embarrass anyone, they know him, the little Jew, dispenser of poisons, servant of debauches, patron of the meretricious, instigator of thieves; he can speak with impunity.

"'See the vulgar palace, where obscene ballerinas caper for the joy of businessmen; the palace where gold triumphs, plastered on the friezes, hanging on the volutes of the capitals, streaming in the grooves, laminating the steps of giant stairways; the palace where lascivious rhythms live, where vile syllables blossom. The carriages of the rich are outside the doors and the leader of the powerful, the Man of the red escutcheon, descends from the royal coach. The little Jew is there; he approaches, bows, his gaze glowering, he brushes the mantle of the man to whom one bows so low: "Are you not weary," he says, "of your concubines? I have the flower that is necessary to reanimate your flesh."

"'The Man of the red escutcheon recoils. Oh, the voice heard! It awakens atavistic echoes in the depths of his memory—those of Sinai, undoubtedly—and the little Jew repeats: "Are you not weary?"'

"'"Is that you, Lord?" cries the Man of the red escutcheon.

"'"It's me. I am the God of whom your spirit dreams. . . ."'

"'Night falls over the joyous stupor of the crowd; the morning illuminates the first day of redemption. Behold the temple of your race, the one in which the pain of the petty and the misfortune of the weak are bought and sold; God is introduced; those fortunate ones shiver with delight on seeing their image. God speaks; it is the language they expect, the one that they announce daily and, in the transport of their enthusiasm, they spread out into the squares and the streets, crying to all those who are waiting: "The Messiah has finally come!"'

"Such," said the Chinaman, "is the story that I was told in India, where the kingdom of Krangamore was built, by an old rabbi versed in the arcana of the Kabbala and confident in the Trinity."

"Do you believe what he announced to you?"

"Have I not said so? Israel will not know its Messiah until he wishes to manifest himself in the only form accessible to its soul."

"And on that day?"

"On that day, be certain that the Christians, who have always had secret sympathies for the practical conduct of the Jews, will be glad to find an honorable pretext, and will convert."

"But what of the wellbeing of humankind?"

"Whatever the form in which God will debase himself in order to seduce humankind, he will be able to lead it to salvation."

In Excelsis

To Leconte de Lisle.

Man is a perfectible animal.
Wisdom.

A *deserted plateau on the highest summit of a mountain. Rocks that no moss softens lie on the ground, devoid of any tree and even any brushwood. Only an intense and vibrant light animates the silence of austere stones and the sun's rays fall direct and terrible, for they are no longer interrupted by the blinds of mists. The sides of the mountain are gripped by pale and fleecy clouds, which unfurl and seem to assail the altitudes. On the plateau, outside a grotto, a man is seated.*

PRIMUS POETA

Ten thousand years ago the last voice announcing the Word was killed, and countless centuries ago, already, my lyre was broken by order of the gods. Again, on the de-flowered earth, the vibrations of the ultimate song reverberate, languid and dying, like the breath of breezes that die away amid the reeds of clear lakes.

Henceforth, my ears will no longer perceive the echoes

that come from below. The chorus of magical syllables has flown away; toward the profound skies it has gone, to rejoin the antique and sororal harmonies. In me, it has resounded, as sonorous as an appeal, as dolorous as a flight. The veiled queens of infinity have ceased to exist in this miserable life, they have conquered the eternal life of ineffable words and radiant ideas.

(He falls silent and meditates, mute, his gaze lost, while the sun declines, sowing tawny flowers on the slopes of the mountain.)

Oh, the first dawn, when the masters of destiny denuded the prodigious essences for me! In the white morning, they appeared, and calmed the rumor of the woods and the pompous plaint of the seas. The air palpitated with unknown intoxications, new perfumes were revealed to my senses, corollas were born and dissolved in the ether; the heavy wall of darkness that cloistered the world collapsed under the finger of the seers, and the first among men, I communicated with the Universe.

(Distant harmonies stir space; the man's face is irradiated, a vibrant swarm of russet bees surrounds his head with a living nimbus. The chorus of voices approaches; it resounds above the mountain. The man listens, ecstatic.)

CHORUS IDEARUM AETERNARUM

The virgins that you possessed, the virgins always immaculate, salute you, first lover, very dear spouse.

PRIMUS POETA

Pure forms, eternal lovers who appeared to me once in the initial dawn, you who have extended your lips to my kisses, you who have given your loins to my embraces, I, the husband of your dilection, salute you, wives.

CHORUS IDEARUM AETERNARUM

Elect, what chagrin is pricking you, the only one of your race who has lived a minute of the true life? You know us and you sing us; under the plectrum, the surging lyre created the world a second time. Immortal Aede who incarnated the Word, unique king of superhuman rhythms, mortal poets have only repeated the syllables sung by you on the unprecedented day of revelations. No word exists that you have not spoken, no vision is evoked that you have not wished. What do you need? Is the glory not sufficient for you of being the veritable father of the initiates who sow your words in the wind of dusks and the mist of dawns?

PRIMUS POETA

Why have the glorious, whom nothing can resist, wanted me to know the terrestrial end of the sages to whom my spirit gave birth?

CHORUS IDEARUM AETERNARUM

The children you engendered have woven the thread that retains you. Only their death can liberate you from life.

PRIMUS POETA

Alas, alas! Seers, behold! Today, the last man who knew my multiple names will die, the last who repeated the noble poems of my sons. With him they will perish; with him I will perish, and now the dolor grips me of losing a vile glory. "Until the day when no mouth repeats your songs and your strophes," said the august Master, "you shall persist." I have groaned at that immutable sentence, but I never believed in the disappearance of the fervent, the death of the priests. In my solitude, I have acquired the most marvelous sciences; will they serve me merely to mourn the hierodule who has broken the last censer?

CHORUS IDEARUM AETERNARUM

That is the irredeemable infirmity attached to the flesh. You have not been able to abdicate its transitory form; in that you are similar to the beings that swarm beneath you like miserable swine, and you know their terrors and you know their woes. Until the hour of deliverance, the struggle will persist.

PRIMUS POETA

The effort is futile. To create harmony, strength is impotent. (*He meditates.*) Do the Gods who incarnate themselves not fall? Is not the impalpable mist that envelops them when they descend toward us sufficient to lower them? And do I, entirely kneaded of mud, want to conserve the spiritual parcel that I have the mission to keep? Alas, I mourn my futile royalty, and the joy of a definitive empire does not console me. I shall live in all and for all; I would like to live alone.

O you, powerful individuals that I invoke one last time, let me sing! Eternal spouses, divest yourselves once more of your shroud of clouds; as on the primordial day, permit my mouth to kiss your forehead. Let my voice descend toward the plains; let the one who is agonizing hear the dear strings vibrate, that the beloved sounds might send him a good slumber.

CHORUS IDEARUM AETERNARUM

Here we are, sweet husband of our dilection, we have come to tender our lips to your kisses. Here our wings of light vibrate around you. Sweet husband, here we are!

(In the air, traversed by harmonious and clear waves, the forms appear, wreathed in glory, clad in radiance. The man contemplates them, dazedly, his tremulous hands extended toward them; then, with a great gesture that accompanies the consenting gaze of the forms, he seizes the golden Lyre. His religious fingers waken the latent sonorities from the long sleep to which destinies have confined them; they fill the air with the divine prelude of their resurrection. The swarm of bees plays around the glorious curve and seems to accompany the moving melodies. The man sings, while the stimulated apparitions lean their foreheads toward him and spread the arachnid gauze of their blonde hair over their shoulders.)

Lake with fresh waters, whose slow waves die away on the squamous strand like sticky entrails drawn from the belly of unknown monsters; lake in which the extinct pupil goes to sleep and which no amicable reflection comes to agitate; sad lake that embraces plains with rugged backs, infertile terrains of inflexible soil, a russet buckler opposed to subterranean seeds; bleak lake, in the midst of your hostile waves I have built the castle of my dreams, the castle where the torch of pride burns on the highest tower.

Marvelous Tower stacking its porphyry terraces, concealing variegated flower beds and orchards forbidden by guardian bees and fountains, jailers of living waters that agitate beneath a carpet of white lotus, breaking their foam on the jasper of prisons; superb Tower, you have closed like eyelids the windows opened over the morose lake by careless architects, and you reserve the welcome of your eyes set in marble for interior gardens embalmed by privet, bright with golden roses. Your attentive stones, Tower, listen to errant and imprisoned voices; your echoes repeat the songs voiced and you make them live again by way of the porticos and the colonnades, in the empty rooms and in the galleries, in the midst of friendly foliage, in the depths of benevolent grottoes clad in the velvet of moss.

O flutes that prelude on the rims of wells, rustic pipes resonating near ponds stirred by the leaps of carp; lutes, rebecs, and you, viols d'amor, gone astray among the charms, the cherished walls perpetuate your melodies. In the chapels, which blue-tint the crimson of stained-glass windows, the plaint of mysterious psalterions is heard, tender nebels and enamored kinnors. But in the vastest and most hidden of your chambers, manor of my sweet dreams, in the chamber perfumed by the sacred balms of marine onyx, on the altar of sardonyx anointed with frank myrrh, stands the royal Lyre, dominatrix and sovereign of the lofty castle of my hopes.

Alas, perpetual palace of rhythms, refuge of oboes and harps in exile, sacred reliquary of puerile cantilenas and glorious strophes, the indifference of the gelatinous waters was stirred one day by the scorn that you affirmed. The lake emerged from its silence and the viscous arms of its waves gripped your perishable foundations tumultuously, proud tower. The army of poisonous plants unsealed the blocks of which your ramparts were proud; the juice of purulent henbanes frayed your cements, the rosy fingers of foxgloves scratched the marbles corroded by the somber umbels of hemlock, the army of fungus and mildew bit into the beams, while the complicit wind agitated the violet berries of the powerful henbanes, an assailing host of minuscule battering rams smashing the walls.

You vacillate, castle of sonorous visions; the arch of your vaults buckles, your turrets collapse, your gardens die, your limpid pools darken, and soon the sticky waters, victorious, will extend over what was you the dull shroud of their dismal waves, their waves of oblivion.

(The man looks down. The thick layer of clouds folds up in snowy spirals and a city becomes visible, profiling its obelisks and rounding its cupolas, its uniform streets converging on a large square where a tumultuous crowd is gathered. In the square is a platform,

*and on the platform a throne: the leader of the people
is seated there surrounded by old men; heralds are in
the four corners holding brass trumpets. Opposite the
platform, on the other side of the square, is a low
house whose unexpected style contrasts with the surrounding dwellings. The vestibule of the house opens
to a single, enormous room. It is filled with paintings,
statues, precious gold plate, rare furniture and musical instruments of outdated forms. In the middle is a
low bed, covered with fabrics whose tissue in enlaced
with gems. An ephebe clad in scarlet silk is lying
on the bed; a halting breath agitates his breast with
somersaults; he is dying, but his face, of translucent
alabaster, is radiant with joy; he is listening, his gaze
lost, and the lustral gleams of the setting sun bathe
the curtains and sheets of the bed. From above, the
man sees everything.)*

PRIMUS POETA

Plaintive hierodule, it was your soul, the beautiful castle
of my hopes, your voice was the echo of its vaults, your
heart the fresh bed of its flowers. Your mouth, you who
are dying, sang the loss of eternal verses, and your agony
is their terrestrial agony, plaintive hierodule, you whom
the venom of insults and the poison of hatred is killing,
plaintive hierodule, you who are dying.

ULTIMUS HIEROPHANTA

Sovereign mothers, of whom I am the ultimate servant, you have heard my reverent voice, and the eldest of
your sons, the Mediator King, salutes the tomb impending

for me, bringing the light. Mysterious, revelatory Death advances, benevolent Death, auxiliary of salvation.

The exile is concluded, life approaches; the pale horse that she rides comes to whinny at my threshold. She has broken the seal of morose days with the hooves of her horse, and the nocturnal cloak gemmed with stars is torn under the imminent breath of the limitless day.

(On the square, the crowd is noisy and menacing; clamors are heard that reach the moribund.)

TURBA

So long as the Enemy lives, wellbeing will flee our dwellings, the calm wellbeing that our forefathers predicted, the wellbeing that had dissimulated those who were initially called poets, those who were named hierophants for a long time. We live in anguish and fear, and we close our doors, for we fear for our sons the echo of the last lying voice. When, without constraint, shall we live freely, the life of placid joys, before served tables, next to beds of amour and repose? Why not, powerful and tutelary chiefs, accord us the torture of the man who wants to dream far away from us?

(The old men, shaken by a frisson of terror, rise to their feet in tumult.)

SENATORES

To dream! Who uttered that word and that blasphemy? No one dreams, stupid crowd; the Dream is dead *(they stammer in a senile fashion and announce:)* The Dream is dead!

DUX POPULI

Children, give free rein to the natural powers that our sages have been able to tame; they are liberating, and henceforth, they will work for you. I know that there are among you, people, intrepid hearts whom no action frightens, but allow Death to preserve weak and fearful souls from possible remorse.

ULTIMUS HIEROPHANTA

The work is done, you who surround me, calm your impatience; you will soon be alone! Alone, for the harmony of the great woods agitated by the breath of evening and the murmur of the sea stimulated by the morning star will no longer exist, there being no ear to hear them. Sound will perish, no voice any longer uttering rhythms; light will be extinguished, no eye any longer capturing it. Sparse voices, floating radiance that surround my couch, you will flee with me, and the echo of the last words will be abolished, reflections dissolved in conclusive glimmers. Fatal Dioscuri, profound Night, and you, obscure Silence, unique and double power, come toward them; your tread has brushed the ground, which has not trembled; oh, the tread of Night and that of Silence, which I alone heard here!

PRIMUS POETA

Do not listen to the hostile tumult that unfurls around you, when the temporary bonds are broken, when my saving appeal comes to you. You are the victim who preserves me from temptations, the holocaust that frees me from regrets. By me you were, by you I shall be and by us you shall be. Thus will be accomplished the triple mystery sealed by the gods at the dawn of time.

(In the square, the clamors of the crowd have fallen silent; the leader of the people, still standing on the platform, stares at the house of death. Suddenly, a soldier cuts through the crowd; he climbs the steps and he murmurs a few words in the ear of the chief, whose laureate head inclines. At a gesture, the heralds put their trumpets to their mouths, and the brass reso-nates; they fall silent, and the chief advances.)

DUX POPULI

The hour has come, elders, the hour so long awaited by you, the hour for which you were impatient, people!

TURBA

The hour has come, glory to the hour of joy!

(In the empyrean, a troop of angels ascends toward the heavens; the Hierophant sees them.)

CHORUS ANGELORUM

The hour has come, Alleluia!

PRIMUS POETA and ULTIMUS HIEROPHANTA

Alleluia, the hour has come! Alleluia!

DUX POPULI

The new era is opening and the illusory dream is flying far away from you forever.

SENATORES (*stammering.*)

The dream is dead, the dream is dead.

DUX POPULI

The Dream is going away to die. Fortunate our sons, fortunate, they shall know the good delights, those that no one thinks tedious, untroubled by morose and deceptive visions. The last disciple of the lying creators of dreams and images is agonizing in his solitude, and his death is finally giving us the true life. When this day has elapsed, the aedes will have ceased to be, and, if the distant fatherland they delighted in exalting was so tender to their eyes, they ought to be joyful. And we too are joyful! Our legends tell that when one of those divine men—thus they called themselves, and thus their credulous victims saluted them—disappeared, the bells rang with funereal accords, mingling brazen tears with the sobs of the mourners.

SENATORES

The bells are broken, they have fled the sounds of fear. We have heard them, alas. Will they ever be reborn, the bells whose tongues have been torn out?

DUX POPULI

No, Venerable ones, the bells, mutilated dogs, have fallen silent forever.

CHORUS CAMPANARUM

Glory and triumph! Hosanna to the queens of eternity! The Absolute shivers, toward him the supreme emanation is returning! Holy soul, listen to the last plaint of the body you are deserting. Glory and joy! Infinite, come to Infinity!

ULTIMUS HIEROPHANTA

Hosanna! Virgins of pure metal that impenitent Faust feared in his solitude; gentle martyrs to the mouth violated by humans, you who have received reconquered Faust on the edge of sidereal enclosures! Hosanna, evocative messengers of paternal dilections.

DUX POPULI

Our heralds, for the last time, will make the brass of clarions resound; for the last time, for it is good that even those voices cease to be heard.

(The heralds put the trumpets to their mouths and blow.)

TURBA

Triumph and glory of our accomplished wishes.

DUX POPULI

We have vanquished the jailers of frank spasms, the possessors of fearless intoxications, and now we no longer hear their songs, somber spoilers of the real. Disappeared are those who knew the philters of despair, those who created the intangible phantoms and the gods of fear, cruel for the flesh. Disappeared are those who polluted Amour and the embrace, the unique delight, the sole reality, and made the suffering of the impossible and deceptive desire. (*He turns toward the elders.*) You have known the terror of the dream; we have been indifferent to it; our children will have forgotten it.

PRIMUS POETA (*He sees and hears everything.*)

Eternal lovers, pure forms, who appeared to me long ago in the initial dawn, liberate me and liberate him, the one who is suffering and dying.

CHORUS IDEARUM AETERNARUM

The children you conceived, aedes and the pious, to whom you imparted your soul, are the obstacles to your wishes. Death alone can undo the weft.

CHORUS CAMPANARUM

Death hastens, her bright wings fill space; she carries the balm, the balm of life.

ULTIMUS HIEROPHANTA

Pastoral sister, I perceive your light. Voices are calling me toward the real.

CHORUS ANGELORUM

Death liberates! Here is Death, daughter of God.

(In the square, a second messenger arrives. He climbs the steps of the platform and speaks to the Dux, whose face is radiant.)

DUX POPULI

The work is finished; the accursed race has sunk into darkness; the new and much anticipated race is born to daylight; the human race is delivered from the dream. People, salute your liberators.

TURBA

The free Life, the Life that we know how to live, the Life that death cannot vanquish.

(A cortege advances, following a woman who presents two infants to the crowd. Cries of enthusiasm burst forth, echoing all the way to the most distant horizons, and they swell to a tempest when the Dux seizes the infants and holds them up to the heavens. The entire people can see them; they are two apes. The elders rise to their feet tumultuously and run forward.)

SENATORES

Behold salvation! Fortunate our extinct eyes, which can
close henceforth; behold salvation!

DUX POPULI and TURBA

Behold salvation! Alleluia!

> *(The walls of the house in which the Hierophant is
> agonizing split apart; he sees the apotheosis and sits
> up, haggard.)*

ULTIMUS HIEROPHANTA

Night, sovereign Night has conquered their souls.

CHORUS IDEARUM AETERNARUM

They are dying forever and they think they are reborn;
the veils around them are thickening and they think they
can see the light; they are sinking into oblivion and they
believe they are within reach of wellbeing. They are abandoning the royal way, they are chasing away the healing
and mild essences, they are being born for dolor and grim
fear; the extended gesture of our hands is withdrawn
from them. And you, the beloved, come toward infallible
glories.

PRIMUS POETA

Come, my son.

CHORUS IDEARUM AETERNARUM, CHORUS ANGELORUM, CHORUS CAMPANARUM

You are renouncing base and transitory forms, you are affranchised from the abject earth; the hour of deliverance has sounded. The blissful life is near; flee Egypt and let this be the exodus of virtue. Alleluia! The hour has come, Alleluia!

(The Poet King descends, followed by divine choirs, preceded by russet messenger bees. The Hierophant extends his hands toward the cohort, and Death appears, virginal and beautiful, wreathed in myrtle.)

ULTIMUS HIEROPHANTA

Behold the day! (*He dies.*)

(At that moment, in the square, a herald throws a torch into the house of the Hierophant, and the devastating flame consumes the works preserved by the piety of the last servant.)

CHORUS IDEARUM AETERNARUM

Toward our Father we uncreated climb again, toward the Absolute, toward the Light, toward the Uncreated. Captives of the houses of distress, we escape the enemy hands.

PRIMUS POETA

Come to me, my sovereign daughters.

ULTIMUS HIEROPHANTA

Come to me, O mothers of mildness.

CHORUS IDEARUM AETERNARUM

Our lost sisters, come to us.

PRIMUS POETA, ULTIMUS HIEROPHANTA and
CHOREGORUM PERSONAE

Let us go to *Him*.

The Forest

Listen; the forest, in the distance, out there, is stirring. . . .
F. Vielé-Griffin.

SAD soul, disappointed heart, infatuated with divine chimeras that gallop in skies reddened by inviolate dawns or misted by tender dusks, you have crossed the threshold and your intrepid feet will not hesitate. The virginal and annunciatory virtues are summoning you, and you come, plaintive heart, weary soul.

You come, you enter, treading the parvis of sardonyx incrusted with magical carbuncles, and behind you, the door closes with an evocative sound. You feel distant from the hostile world, far from the unhealthy words that have afflicted your morose heart and your wounded soul excessively.

You believed yourself to be liberated, and, proud of your courage, you sang the paean in honor of the spinners who attracted you; but you searched for them in vain, with an emotional soul and an impatient heart. Alone, before you, the lugubrious forest extended, the forest saddened by the absence of familiar birds and sylvan nymphs, the bushy and empty forest, the forest filled with trees and strange flowers, the forest populated by imprisoned spirits.

The songs that incited you still resonated, but distant and vague, and one might have thought them a supernatural choir of virgins descending unperceived hills. Then, guided by the beloved sounds, you penetrated into the thickets to vanquish the unruly brambles, and, face and hands bloody, you advanced, heart resolute and soul strong.

Suddenly, the shroud of silence fell away, the wood became animated; your closed ears opened, you heard the murmur of the foliage, the clamor of oaks, the wailing of moss, the quivering of reeds, the rumor of privet and laurier-roses, the cantilena of giant lilies and bright jasmines. You heard the hymn uttered:

"Fraternal traveler expelled by the crowds, adventurous fugitive, we salute you. You have recognized the vanity of terrestrial glories; you have shamed the banal ambition of men, the ambition that conquers treasons and felonies dearly. Be saluted, hero! We welcome you at the entrance to your new dwellings, as faithful servants welcome an expected master, and also as hierophants seated on the steps of a temple to instruct ignorant mystes. Listen, we are the initiators.

"You have lived in the midst of barbarians, and the dream captive in your being, the dream remembering lost lands, rendered the roads familiar to all dolorous to you. While the nocturnal words of those who triumph rang in your ears you went forth, without hearing them; in the desert of your senses shone friendly torches, and you followed the dear scorned gleams. But you alone saw them and our friends accused you of folly, and our mother withdrew from you, and the indifferent sniggered, for you marched with your head held high, your lips speaking.

"One evening when, weary of insults, your face soiled with mud, your limbs bruised by stones, you had sat down on the edge of a ditch, you saw white phantoms coming toward you in the repopulated fields; they dressed you in rich fabrics, they sprinkled you with precious perfumes, they delighted you with specious and promising words, and you came toward the doors that closed the Avalons and the Thules. The guardian monsters crouched down, and the sigillary emerald, touched by fearless fingers, allowed you to enter the gardens that you believed to be pleasant.

"Now, here you are, pilgrim whose soul is shivering and whose heart is emotional. You await the forms that haunt you, the ideas, mothers and queens, that you want to conquer. Alas, they will flee, illusory princesses, and you will rediscover the rancor of former days. Eternal fugitive of appearances, you will always see them surging forth before your eyes, and the visions, which alone are real, will perpetually fly away, beyond your reach, mysterious doves escaping the grasp of the bird-catcher. Remain with us, do not continue your route; we will give you the only real wellbeing: the death of dreams. Stay. You will go to sleep in the serene peace of ignorance, in the delectable abolition of desires, and fervent roses will make you a bed of repose and forgetfulness."

As you once paused at the crossroads of cities, seduced by the sound of lyres scattered for you in the air, you pause here, persuaded by the insidious voices. The poisonous aroma of the trees penetrates you with weakness, your knees flex and, voluntarily, you are inclining toward the bunch of enticing corollas, when once again you perceive the fading chorus of spinning maidens:

"Hear us, undervalued of the world; beware of murderous lakes. Vanquisher of dragons and wyverns, beware of more subtle enemies."

At the supreme appeal the scales fall from your eyes. You see; you recognize those who are retaining you. The branches of the oaks are flourishing bitter hands, the boughs of the beeches are sharpening rigid claws, the calices of the flowers are stirring perverse mouths, their pistils capped with sly pupils, heavy tresses are agitating on the foreheads of elms, the willows are bending their trunks into redoubtable rumps, and the mosses are starry with white breasts and red fleeces.

"Recognize them," clamor the spinners. "The ancient adversaries, the false servants of the Word, the killers of the ideal, the lovers of vanities, the worshipers of the beast, the glorifiers of metal and flesh. They believe they have won reliable delights, and the living who salute them celebrate them as fortunate initiates. But even if they were able to cross the walls, as felons, the plains of mysterious Avalons and white Thules would be forever closed to them. Courage, O vagabond of mortal life; triumph over the last ambushes; come to us. The golden sistra are ready, the strings vibrating under the plectrum, the air quivering with latent words, rhythms are dormant in the wind, thoughts are gathering in the depths of grottoes. Come, you will waken this world, which is waiting for you."

And, reanimated by the divine sisters, you traverse the thickets with a firm tread. You extract yourself from the languorous lianas, the voluptuous appeal of the crimsoned rose-bushes, and you finally see the supernatural lawns shining, and the solemn lakes blossoming, beneath the purifying light of the revelatory sky.

A PARTIAL LIST OF SNUGGLY BOOKS

LÉON BLOY *The Tarantulas' Parlor and Other Unkind Tales*

FÉLICIEN CHAMPSAUR *The Latin Orgy*

BRENDAN CONNELL *Metrophilias*

QUENTIN S. CRISP *Blue on Blue*

QUENTIN S. CRISP *September*

LADY DILKE *The Outcast Spirit and Other Stories*

BERIT ELLINGSEN *Vessel and Solsvart*

RHYS HUGHES *Cloud Farming in Wales*

JUSTIN ISIS *Divorce Procedures for the Hairdressers of a Metallic and Inconstant Goddess*

VICTOR JOLY *The Unknown Collaborator and Other Legendary Tales*

JEAN LORRAIN *Masks in the Tapestry*

JEAN LORRAIN *Nightmares of an Ether-Drinker*

JEAN LORRAIN *The Soul-Drinker and Other Decadent Fantasies*

CATULLE MENDÈS *Bluebirds*

KRISTINE ONG MUSLIM *Butterfly Dream*

YARROW PAISLEY *Mendicant City*

DAVID RIX *A Suite in Four Windows*

FREDERICK ROLFE *An Ossuary of the North Lagoon and Other Stories*

JASON ROLFE *An Archive of Human Nonsense*

TOADHOUSE *Gone Fishing with Samy Rosenstock*

TOADHOUSE *Living and Dying in a Mind Field*